FINDING LOVE

Storms and Happy Endings

By

J L Appleton

Copyright © Jasmine Appleton 2018

www.jasmine-appleton.co.uk
And at Amazon Books

Chapter One	Mollie
Chapter Two	Grace and Josh
Chapter Three	Beth
Chapter Four	Stormy Times
Chapter Five	Coffee Shop
Chapter Six	Grace and Josh
Chapter Seven	Beth and Andy
Chapter Eight	Mollie and ?
Chapter Nine	Hospital
Chapter Ten	Another meeting of three
Chapter Eleven	Love
Chapter Twelve	The next morning
Chapter Thirteen	Beth and Barney. A dog's Love
Chapter Fourteen	Emotional love
Chapter Fifteen	A week away
Chapter Sixteen	Interfering Mollie
Chapter Seventeen	A mix of people
Chapter Eighteen	Hospital gossip
Chapter Nineteen	Say goodbye

Chapter Twenty	A sad day
Chapter Twenty One	A coffee shop meeting
Chapter Twenty Two	Beth needs to find Mollie
Chapter Twenty Three	Weddings

Chapter One
Mollie

Mollie's plane was coming in to land. She hated this part of her journey, would it ever stop in time, before the runway ended? She closed her eyes and tried to find a few happy thoughts. She remembered back to that Spanish beach. She'd taken at short notice a girlie break with Chloe and a couple of other friends from the office, over that long weekend. They had had a laugh, a little too much Sangria and plenty of paella which reminded her, she needed to go on yet another diet.

She thought of the older man on the beach being told by his wife to keep his t-shirt on at his age. He was having none of it and quickly removed the garment over his balding head. Standing upright, he had breathed in deeply to try and hold in his rounded belly, perhaps he had eaten too much Spanish food too. He had no six pack to admire, that was for sure and Mollie had had to look away and cover her mouth to stop a giggle which was trying to escape.

She celebrated her 34th birthday out there, lay on a sunbed and dreamed of meeting a man while on that sun-drenched beach and of falling in love. She wanted this so badly before she hit 40. Oh, dear 40! Her clock was ticking, she wanted a family too but really wanted a husband first; she was old fashioned like that.

Her friends at work told her on her thirtieth not to worry, it's only a number. It was all right for them, they were still under 30, she had already moved on another four years.

Mollie wanted someone to spend the rest of her life with; she almost had it once with Paul an up and coming doctor, but she had thrown him away, a few years ago. She opened her eyes and let out a sigh as the plane banked to the left for its second attempt.

Most of her girlfriends wanted high-powered jobs with the big wage packet that came with that and to leave children to very much later, but Mollie dreamed of settling down. Of course, there was always Ben, her life long friend, and she sighed again.

The plane shuddered from turbulence and Mollie screwed her eyes up tightly, remembering the storm the weather forecasters talked of before she left home, the remnants of a Caribbean hurricane which may hit the country on her return.

She tried not to think of that and let her mind drift back to boyfriends past; she hadn't had many. She thought of Ben again. He had declared his love for her on many occasions over the years. Even in school, but he did nothing for her in the love department, even though they had been out a few times. He would always just be a good friend, like a brother looking out for her. He was very good looking and kind, but he wasn't for her.

Recently Mollie thought she had met the man of her dreams, in the new office manager. Michael swept in from America like a breath of fresh air, tall, dark-haired and with a short well-kept beard to his smiling face. He was a smart Englishman who had been working in the New York office for a couple of years. He returned home after a tragedy hit his family, so she heard on the company grapevine.

He had taken all the girls at work by surprise and most loved him in some way or another, other than Victoria who announced to Mollie in a very loud voice, so all her work colleagues could hear: 'he is married, to another man, you know.'

"No," Mollie gasped and nearly choked on the water she'd taken from the cooler outside the office door. Victoria tried to dodge the water which Mollie couldn't help but spit out over Victoria's black pristine suit.

"Oops, sorry," Mollie declared as she walked away with a little smirk to her face, something she rarely did.

Victoria always managed to bring the worst out in people. Her popularity with the other girls was low since the day she arrived to take the position of Michael's assistant earlier that year. She thought herself above the rest as she sat at her desk alongside his office, tapping her keyboard, while facing the rest of the team at their desks.

Victoria had not been impressed at Mollie's mishap and she'd taken a tissue to dab at the wet spots on the material of her expensive looking jacket.

"Haven't you seen the wedding ring on his finger?" Victoria carried on while Mollie moved away. Victoria's depressive tone followed Mollie. Victoria was always happy to make someone else unhappy. Mollie's heart had sunk at the time, because no, she hadn't noticed the ring; she was too busy looking into his green eyes and daydreaming.

Once Mollie called her Vicky and had been told in no uncertain terms, her name was, '***Victoria***'.

Victoria had arrived under a cloud of intrigue, as told by gossip leaked from Human Resources; the grapevine was working well. The source of this gossip had seen a note explaining that Victoria had been sent packing from her last place of work in London after an incident of which she could not speak and soon she become the office bitch, if not a witch as Chloe called her.

"Bit old for that hairdo," one of the other girls had commented under her breath, after she felt Victoria's spitiful side.

Mollie saw her as a strutting peacock in her black patent leather, high heeled shoes, dark suit and huge colourful beads about her neck. Bright red lipstick matched her long pointed nails, or were they talons ready to strike? A long black coat covered that black trouser suit and white blouse. Chloe said she only needed a broomstick and a pointed hat to cover her black ponytail which swung back and forth as she stalked into the building on her first day before marching around their office. Her skin looked grey from the pale face powder slapped on close around the dark grey eye shadow, applied above long false eyelashes which all made for a ghostly look. Her beak-like nose stuck out from a head held high and it was soon stuck into everyone else's business.

Mollie had been the first to notice her interfering ways but was too polite to say. The other girls voiced their opinions in the office and it soon became clear Victoria was not going to fit in.

Michael, their new boss, did though and very quickly. He came across as a kind and fair man just like Mollie's father who had suddenly died after a long illness and the reason for her return a day earlier than her friends. A tear crept from Mollie's eye as the plane's wheels hit the tarmac. She was home and wrenched from her thoughts. As the plane taxied around to park up, she knew she had a funeral to arrange.

Her father had been a happy man in life, or so it seemed to Mollie, always smiling and cheerful. He was thoughtful and kind to his daughter. A well-dressed man in shirt and tie, even when sitting in his chair at home after his early retirement. He would have taken charge of any situation which might arise in life and kept Mollie safe, that was until he was taken ill of course.

Michael came across in the same way, taking charge in a caring unbiased way for all his staff, not like the manager before him. Oh, Judith, she almost split the team in two and only half the work got completed in any one day, ghastly woman and now there was Victoria.

The plane gave a jolt and came to a standstill. Mollie returned to reality. Her father had died, she hadn't expected that when she left home for the sun and now she had arrived into the rain of England, back to help her mother sort things out.

She released her seat belt to move to collect her overhead luggage. A man reached up to help her; it was Michael. Her heart jumped, her cheeks flushed and she caught her breath before speaking.

"What are you doing on this flight?" She was surprised to see him.

"Been out to Spain on business," he replied and stood back to let her walk forward.

Mollie felt her insides turn over before she took a quick look back. Michael seemed to be on his own and was looking right at her. She felt nervous, silly, like a teenager. She almost stumbled down the stairs leading from the plane to the tarmac which was wet and slippy from the drizzle. Walking from the baggage claim area, Mollie turned to see Michael a few metres in front and she followed. She wanted to catch him up, perhaps bump into him, accidentally of course. But when she found herself outside to hail a taxi she saw him getting into a chauffeur driven car, while a man in a smart suit and cap placed Michael's bags in the boot. Mollie stood still, unsure of what she was seeing. After all, he was only the office manager.

Taking a taxi home she opened the window and felt the still, humid air, as though a storm was building; it was unusual for the time of year. A hurricane was a bit of an exaggeration, she thought for England's south coast. Then again the forecasters had said it was supposed to miss the country by miles and anyway it would have blown itself out by the time it reached England.

Mollie might not have her father to protect her now, but if she happened to be at work when a storm or hurricane hit she would have Michael, he could be her hero. Mollie occasionally fantasized about having a hero; a knight in shining armour rushing in on a white horse to save her. She would often blush at her childish thoughts. Shame it couldn't be Michael, she thought as she arrived at her front door and paused before placing her key in the lock.

After enjoying a welcome cup of English tea with her mother, Margaret, she decided an early night was required. Tomorrow she would go to the shops to buy a raincoat for the bad weather reported to be arriving around lunch time the next day.

It was still far too warm to wear a coat and her jackets were too short, so any excuse to shop made her happy and would take her mind off the not so nice things she had to organize for her late father.

But first, she turned on her laptop which she had purposely left at home. It was time to catch up on her E-mails. There were many messages; where to start? She wriggled herself between her pillows and got comfy. The one she opened first, was from Ben.

"Hi, Mollie, fancy lunch when you're back from Spain?"

"Oh, dear," Mollie mumbled to herself. What was she to say to him?

"Talk later." That was enough for now.

She found Ben's kindness tiresome on some occasions, but she didn't want him, she wanted love, the sort of love that took her breath away, made her flutter inside, made her knees go weak, her head spin. She wanted all-consuming love; she would wait for Mr Right. Hopefully, she wouldn't have to wait too much longer.

"Oh, Michael," she whispered to herself. "If only."

She'd been kissed on the lips by Ben and felt nothing, so it was unlikly to ever happen again after she had asked him not to do that and quickly kissed him on his cheek, telling him they were just very good friends. After that day Mollie heard nothing for a couple of weeks and then suddenly he turned up with an enormous bunch of flowers, kissed her on her cheeks and pointed to the card which simply read, '*very good friends*'. Both smiled at each other and life went on as it always had.

'We will see about lunch', the keys were pressed the second message was sent to Ben. She didn't want to encourage him but she didn't want to hurt him either.

***

The following day, Mollie was shopping in a department store for that raincoat and she decided to keep an eye out for a handsome hero as she often did.

She was happy with the beige raincoat with red tartan lining, after trying it on. Deciding to wear it, she refused the paper carrier bag the store assistant offered and asked to have the price tags removed as she paid with her bank card. She would be ready for the rain once she left the store, but not before she visited the men's department.

Ben had asked her to buy a tie for him as he was too busy to go shopping and would be attending the funeral with her, something she still had to finalise with her mother.

Mollie accidentally touched hands with a rather handsome man as they both picked up the same tie. She looked at him and recalled a newspaper article about a couple who met while food shopping in a supermarket one Friday night. They married only months later. Unfortnately a smart young woman came up to him and slid her arm through his. He gave another warm smile at Mollie who felt embarrassed and looked away as the couple moved off together.

An announcement came over the loudspeaker from a woman speaking in a very agitated voice to all staff and customers.

"Please make your way to the basement slowly and carefully. This is for your own protection from the strong winds building outside. Thank you."

And Mollie moved with the small crowd.

Chapter Two
Grace and Josh

Josh pulled from his uniform trouser pocket a small red velvet box; he held it in his trembling hand as he finished breakfast with his long-term girlfriend, Grace. Together they sat in the arrivals lounge of a small airport on the outskirts of this city.

Watching the TV monitor displaying the arrival times, Josh waited for the internal flight to land. During this waiting time he became impatient with himself and decided to use that hour or two to give Grace a surprise, but before he could, he was called away by his superior officer ringing on his mobile phone.

Josh was to escort a prisoner who was being transferred from the far south of England to Scotland. He was already booked on a plane bound for Scotland and had been asked to oversee the prisoner's transfer. He was to attend a week's information/training session on the workings of a prison. He had been offered the role quite recently in that establishment and was able to work there for three months before he needed to commit himself to the new post, which came with a promotion and more money. The money, he thought, would help in his long term plans with Grace, only he still hadn't got around to telling her.

He would be away from her for the whole of that time and although he wasn't happy with the idea, he wasn't sure that she felt the same way. She had been distracted these last few weeks with her own thoughts on a new job for herself. How was he to convince her to wait for him and not take that job, if she was offered it? But why should he have to convince her? If she truly loved him she would go wherever he went. But as yet she hadn't said those three little words, *I love you,* to him, but neither had he, to her.

Leaving Grace sitting at a small round table holding two empty coffee mugs, a plate of crumbs left from her croissants and his partly eaten bacon and egg breakfast, he got up to turn and rush away. Without so much as a goodbye kiss, he had jumped to attention at the voice on the other end of his phone only half turning to wave and smile at her.

"I have to go," were the only words Grace heard as he stood, and he was gone, pushing the red velvet box back into his pocket without asking his question.

Grace watched him dash around a corner, the phone still held to his ear. His fair hair, cut very short, was, as always, hidden under his police cap.

"What was that all about?" Grace muttered to herself.

She should be used to Josh by now, just taking off at a minute's notice, but that made it no less frustrating when he left her for his work.

Like the weather outside, there had been stormy times in their relationship recently because both put their jobs first, before family, friends and each other; they both knew something needed to change.

What was in that box? Grace thought she could guess; after all, it was heart shaped.

But she could be wrong of course. They hadn't discussed marriage, even though they had been together for four years now, but this wasn't exactly the most romantic place for a proposal, was it?

With a deep sigh, Grace stood, straightened her short skirt, carefully draped her beige raincoat with the red tartan lining over her arm. She had paid a lot of money for this coat in a London west end designer store and made sure she left the untidy table to a waitress to clear. Leaving the airport she headed for the shops. Grace knew there was plenty of time to shop and return later to catch her own flight, but would she catch up with Josh before he left? After all Face timing just wasn't the same as touching him, although better than a phone call.

Arriving in the shopping area, Grace saw exactly the dress for her interview, displayed in a shop window. A blue and white polka dot dress which would look great with her red leather designer shoes and the matching handbag she already carried. Grace was so engrossed in admiring her own reflection in the mirror of the changing room when trying on that expensive dress, she didn't hear her phone ringing at the bottom of her large bag.

She loved her fashions and she would buy this dress whatever the cost before going outside with the intention of phoning both Josh to arrange a meeting point in the airport and the company who'd set an interview for the next day, the reason she was flying out that very evening. Grace needed to know what was in that box before they went their separate ways.

The double doors of the store flew back with the howling wind as Grace walked outside. She heard only part of an announcement, as she passed through the doors.

"Please make your way to the basement slowly and carefully. This is for your own protection. Thank you." This was the second announcement of the day to do with the weather.

Having tried to phone Josh with no luck she turned to move back inside, brushing arms with a young girl who was dashing in.

Chapter Three
Beth

Beth Fox had had a morning arguing with her mother, Lisa, before leaving to shop.

Having heard the weather forecast, warning of a dramatic storm to come later that day gave her the best reason to buy a new raincoat, although her mother thought differently and had told her so. '*It's a waste of money, and you don't need to go out in this weather,*' *Lisa had said.*

Ignoring her mother's words, Beth left home shortly afterwards.

"I will be fine," Beth shouted back at her mother, still in her pyjamas.

"Come here, my girl. I know you're meeting up with that boy again," Lisa shrieked.

"Oh, shut up," and Beth slammed the door behind her.

She ignored both mother and weathermen and did her own storming out with an umbrella tucked under her arm, her boots pulled on, leaving her mother to feel sorry for herself. Nothing new there, Beth thought as she trudged along the path in those floppy boots, a size too big because she'd forgotten to pull on her thicker socks and she wasn't going back for them, to give her mother another chance to complain at her. Making her way to the bus which would take her to the shops, Beth realised there were many cross words with her mother these days.

Lisa had stopped going shopping with her daughter, buying attractive clothes which she said she hated trying on, now that she'd put on a little weight. She had also let her hair grow long and often didn't bother to wash it for days, which was so unlike her. Lisa used to be so pretty with her auburn hair cut short and neat; a little makeup applied to her face whenever she left the house. Her daughter had hoped she would be the same when she was her mother's age. But she felt her mother was letting herself fade into middle age and Beth didn't like it.

Standing at the bus stop the rain started to drizzle again and Beth put up her red umbrella, remembering when her mother had given it to her. That was the day she was singing along with the radio as she half pushed and danced with the vacuum cleaner; she was always up bright and early then. How could she get her happy mum back? Beth worried and found it hard to understand this thing called the menopause which she and her young friends had spoken about; her mother hadn't taken Beth's advice, to go and see a doctor.

Beth tossed her worries away as she clambered up the steps of the bus, to sit at the front.

Her mother would calm down, she always did, just as the weather would calm and everything would be back to normal by the time she returned home with her new raincoat. Beth always smiled to herself when thoughts of trying on new clothes came to her.

For the last few years, since about the time Andy came onto the scene, life with her mother had become worse or was that just a coincidence? Beth wasn't sure as she hadn't had many boyfriends; in fact, really only Andy who she could call a romantic relationship. Other boys were just friends at school. But her mother did not approve of any type of boy and certainly not of a man much older than her daughter and she had made this perfectly clear to Beth.

The bus stopped at the shopping centre and Beth stood and looked out of the windows before moving down the stairs. She saw the autumn colours of curling leaves being ripped from the bending branches in the strong winds. Perhaps the gusts were too strong now to open her umbrella. She jumped from the bus and headed to the shops and was happy to forget about everything else in her life, other than meeting Andy later, of course; he was always on her mind.

Beth dashed through the heavy rain and brushed past Grace, who was standing at the side of the shop with her phone to her ear.

"Sorry,"Beth called out, while moving forward.

***

As with many young people, Beth didn't consider anything could possibly go wrong for her and as to the forecaster's storm, well, they always told you the worst was going to happen and it rarely did.

She missed the first announcement in the store and pushed through people walking towards her. On the model directly in front of her and close by the payment counter hung the very raincoat she'd seen in a magazine and she loved it. She found her size on the rail and quickly tried it on. She was so thrilled with this raincoat, which she was going to buy whatever her mother said. She gave a twirl in front of the mirror. Admiring herself, she pulled up the collar which showed a red tartan trim and she pulled the belt in tight to show off her slight figure. The shop assistant came over to her and explained they must go but that she would stop and make the sale, if she was happy to take it unwrapped.

Beth was very pleased to keep on her beige raincoat with the red tartan lining, so long as the tags were removed. With that done the two women ran off to catch up with the people who were heading to the basement.

Chapter Four
Stormy Times

Mollie, Grace and now Beth along with all the other customers and staff were moving down from the higher floors of fashion to the basement, which stored many boxes of shoes and clothes not yet unpacked.

Some people covered their heads in anticipation of glass flying from the windows where spider patterns now formed in the large arched panels holding the family names of this business. The glass was cracking under the strain of the howling wind. Injuries could happen if they were to burst open and the management worried.

Grace sensed the dread which seemed to hang over the people inside, now looking for somewhere to shelter from that wild weather lashing the streets; the storm had arrived and let out its mighty roar after all and so quickly.

Beth joined the moving sea of humans heading towards the hidden staircase, used only by the staff on a daily basis. People were jockeying for space on those stairs leading down to the basement of this old 1920s shop, which still displayed its original features.

Although the weather forecasters predicted a bad storm, they had changed their minds the night before, saying it would miss the country by miles. Consequently, everyone had been taken by surprise when the weather worsened. Had the weathermen got it so very wrong? Worried faces said they had.

The lashing rain turned to hailstones the size of golf balls which were piling up as thick as snow in the gutters before the rain returned, only to be blown horizontally by that building wind. Clouds of different shades of metal greys rolled with the lighter ones, some were trimmed with pink which made them look very angry indeed and all had been gathering overnight to now hang as a menacing blanket above this small city.

The people on their way to work that morning hadn't witnessed such a storm brewing before and were mesmerised by the many shades in the sky.

A late weather warning had been annonced after most people had left home. Few people heard this and those that had, had taken little notice. The presenter with the beaming smile was very reassuring the evening before and dismissed the notion that the storm would hit the country.

Earlier in the day, Beth, while on the bus, had seen a tree ripped from the earth which left its tangled roots to twist with the wind, roots that looked like a heap of brown slithering snakes going nowhere. Now an old beech tree had fallen and crushed a car in the car park next to the bus station. Michael had just stepped from that car. He was on his way to buy lunch. Luckily no one else had been inside the car. The tree was now blocking the car park's entrance. Black slate roof tiles had been ripped off and had flown through the air like a discus at a sports event, a few just missing a group of men and women at the parking ticket machine. Those people automatically ducked, one man, holding his briefcase over his head for protection as Michael ran passed.

Crowds huddled together, in places where they thought they would be safe, as sharp fork lightning cracked into zig-zag lines across the purple-grey sky and thunder rolled inside those menacing clouds. Of course, there were those people who happily took pictures of the sky and shared them on social media.

In the basement, huddled in a corner, Mollie used her new raincoat much like a security blanket, pulling it close around her.

As the storm reached its peak, Grace and Beth had been pushed closer to Mollie as other groups of women, men, and a few children used up the space around them and the storm raged on.

All three women managed a slight smile, to acknowledge each other, but said nothing. All were thinking, '*she's wearing my coat!*' The stuff of nightmares, for most women, Grace thought as she narrowed her eyes and looked from one to the other; she knew her raincoat was far more expensive than the other two put together.

Mollie, the dreamer made light of the raincoats in her mind. After all, in the great scheme of things, did it really matter?

And Beth, well she felt in her raincoat pocket to be sure she still had the receipt. As soon as they were back upstairs, she intended to exchange it for something a bit more suited to her age group. She wouldn't be seen dead in it again after seeing these two older women in the same coat.

An enormous crack of thunder shook the building; a bolt of lightning must have struck somewhere nearby. Children cried and a couple of very young teenagers squealed.

"Dear God, we're all going to die?" a woman screamed.

Silence fell across this basement of people as an uneasy calm seemed to spread all around. The thunder stopped and some wondered if they should leave and try to get home.

Beth was going to talk to her mother when she returned home, about how she'd changed and then there was Andy; he too required a discussion. She had to make her mother realise she loved him. Beth frowned, as she wondered how she could do that.

Mollie, well she still wanted her hero to appear, and she smiled slightly to herself; perhaps her hero was working in this storm, helping people; yes that's where she would find a hero.

Grace was pushing her fingers through her short blonde, bob haircut and knew she had to return to the airport. She just needed to see Josh and now found an urgency was taking her over, she became fidgety. How did she feel about Josh? What was in that little red velvet box?

Both Josh and Grace needed to catch planes that evening, him to escort his prisoner and her to fly to that all important interview, a job with great prospects, the job she thought she really wanted. It would take her to another city, away from the people she'd grown up with, people who now she was tired of. She felt she had outgrown her shallow life but how would Josh feel about a move from his childhood home to where she wanted to work and not Scotland? He had lived just around the corner to Grace, in the next street in fact, but they hadn't met until they went to work, him in the force and her as an aide to the personal assistant to the commander, in that same building. If she was successful now, she would become a personal assistant herself. Then there was Josh's promotion, his career. Oh dear, she thought, careers could pull relationships apart.

Another thought quickly entered Grace's mind. She wondered, would the airport still be operational when she returned? If her flight was cancelled, she would miss her interview. She frowned now for two reasons; one, did she really want to be with Josh in his new life? Second, an image of that tiny box had shown itself in her mind and that frightened her too. All she could think of was her future, and if she was right about the contents of that little box, did she want to accept it?

"Oh hell," she muttered.

Mollie and Beth heard Grace's words and sent a reassuring half-smile over towards her.

Mollie was the closest to Grace and gently touched her arm to reassure her, thinking she was worried about the storm.

But it was Josh who niggled her, when he left her sitting at the table and in turn, she had headed out shopping. That always made Grace feel good, but was she now going to place a job before him?

The new dress, to wear and impress at her forthcoming interview now lay inside the brown paper bag with the shop's name written in bold gold letters across each side. She held it firmly to her chest as she waited and worried about the storms in her life and the storm outside. Grace glanced at the two women across from her. Both wore raincoats exactly the same as hers. Grace really wasn't happy about that. In her world she wore the best of all the different designs. She studied the faces of these two women close up. One appeared to give the look of a dreamer, a kind person with smiling blue eyes and long blonde hair, who now looked across at Grace and smiled all the more.

Mollie was wondering if she had a handsome hero in her life, or a mother telling her she didn't need a man, unless he was loaded with cash, adding it was about time she found that rich man, now she was in her mid thirties.

"Money's not everything," Mollie told her mother and she remembered the conversation only too well. '*It helps,*' her mother always said. *'Men are only after one thing and then there is the washing, ironing, cleaning, and cooking, of course.'*

'But mother, you like cooking,' Mollie had reminded her.

Mollie carried on daydreaming, trying to push what was happening outside in the street away, just like the time she landed in a plane. Her mother hadn't had an easy life, what with her own father being an alcoholic and then her husband becoming ill while still so young, before enforced retirement came. But Mollie always loved her father and had seen no wrong in him; had she been a fool to think him perfect all those years? He didn't complain of his suffering to his daughter but maybe he continually complained to his wife. Was it that which had dragged her down, made her old before her time? Mollie understood the love between a daughter and a parent was very different to that of husband and his wife, so did her mother suffer too, in a very different way? She needed to know more from her mother about their relationship but that would have to wait until after her father's funeral. Mollie was still cross to think he passed away while she had been away on that girlie weekend abroad enjoying herself. She wouldn't have gone with Chloe if she'd realised death was so close. Then another rumble of thunder brought her back to her situation right now.

Grace caught the eye of Beth, the young girl sitting to her right who was fiddling with her mobile phone, which still found no signal whichever way she held it.

"The damn thing isn't working," Beth mumbled but she kept trying to call her boyfriend, Andy, to ask him to come and find her.

People were becoming unsettled at the thought of drowning, after someone mentioned rather loudly that the river was close by and a few people had seen it rising fast earlier that morning. The once silent basement was turning to mutterings of unrest. No one knew what was going on above ground.

"We need to be higher up this building," Mollie suddenly burst out to anyone who would listen. Her daydreaming turned into a grim image of drowning and she began to panic. Her hope of a hero arriving to save her had vanished.

Grace could see water trickling down the basement steps and reached out to take Mollie's hand, to reassure her everything would be alright.

"Come on," Grace demanded, taking charge of the situation. "We have to get out of here."

Mollie could hardly say a word as she looked in fear at the steps and the other two women in raincoats linked arms to pull her up, ready to walk off.

"I mean to say, as if our country could be hit by a hurricane?" A well-spoken gentleman declared, from across the floor. "It's absurd. Our little part of England gets all sorts of weather, but a hurricane?"

People turned to look at this white-haired, tall man wearing a dark pinstripe suit and waving a long, thin, rolled up, black umbrella, which he used to point to the way out.

"Follow me," he commanded with a voice of authority.

A few people did, they thought he sounded and looked like an ex-army officer standing upright and in charge.

Grace pulled at the young woman standing next to her who still watched her phone, waiting for a light, a message, anything.

"What's your name?" Grace asked as they walked forward. "I'm Grace."

Grace smiled at both women, one either side of her.

"Mollie."

"And I'm Beth." She looked up from her phone for the first time. She was the youngest of the three. Pushing the phone into her raincoat pocket she felt the receipt rolled up and remembered she needed to exchange her raincoat as soon as possible.

The water was now pouring down the basement steps and people were beginning to run.

The three women eased themselves along together, safety in numbers they all seemed to be thinking, someone looking out for you was always a good thing. Somehow they managed to work their way through those anxious people who were shoving others up the stairs. People noticed the water turning from a trickle into what was now quite a gush around their feet. The three stopped for a moment as Mollie helped a fallen child to its feet before being pushed along once again as the water turned into a waterfall. Word quickly spread of a flood coming, leaving people panicking about getting out, making them push all the more.

"It's the river. What shall we do?" a young woman called out in despair.

"It must have burst its banks," another older woman's voice was heard to shout.

Panic hung in the still humid air; it was like a dampness that floated about their heads with a smell that Beth remembered from her school bus days when she first saw Andy.

Andy was the young man who had caused yet another argument between her and her mother that very morning. She had no idea what the atmosphere would be like when she got home. Hot and hostile, most likely, not cool and calm, Beth was sure of that, but she was not giving Andy up.

"I'm almost nineteen now and will soon be out to work full-time," she muttered under her breath.

Grace asked her what she had said.

"Oh, nothing of importance," Beth replied and carried on walking with the crowd, determined to be safe. She didn't have any more time to worry about her mother or Andy; she needed to keep hold of Grace's raincoat.

Behind her came Mollie clinging onto the tail of Beth's raincoat.

The three women had lost hold of each other's arms and now ended up trailing behind each other, holding raincoat tails. How bizarre; three complete strangers meeting and wearing raincoats of the same style, Beth thought, while Mollie thought it was a sign, of what she didn't really know yet. She was a Piscean, the star sign of the two fishes swimming in opposite directions, which said it all about her. She found it difficult to make a decision. She was a great believer in signs, destiny, and her dreams of course, which she often voiced to her close friend Chloe.

Suddenly all three found themselves on the ground floor where children were stamping in the water, having great fun while parents wore their worried faces and told their little ones to stop it, as they hung tightly to their hands.

"Wait for me," friends called after each other.

Tall men were looking over shoulders of others, trying to reach wives or girlfriends. The basement had been left behind and now the three women stood on the pavement to see the river did not burst its banks, it was purely the amount of rain that had fallen in such a short space of time and ran down those steps.

People walked in boots and shoes sodden by the murky flood water rippling slowly all around, water which now started to subside as calm was beginning to settle within those crowds. Items in the storeroom floated by the last of those worried people who were still struggling to get up the stairs, while on the top-floor, the wind had blown in some of those beautiful panes of glass. Glass crunched under the feet of staff checking for damage.

The three women stood together in the doorway of the store.

"I need a coffee fix. Do you think it's safe to go outside?" Grace asked hopefully as she poked her head out from under the shop's canopy, which offloaded its cold water in droplets down her neck.

"Oh!" she cried and wiped at her wet skin with her hand.

"I think we should wait a bit," answered Mollie, loitering in the doorway, not sure whether to move out or not.

"Come on," Beth yelled and pushed her way forward. "Let's go."

A typical youngster, she has no fear, Grace thought.

"Come on then, let's make a run for it. There's a cafe just down on the corner," Beth called back as she made a sudden dash out into the rain.

Splashing through standing puddles of water, her boots sending water sprays into the air she stamped along, quietly enjoying her childish antics. The other two caught up with her and, arm in arm with umbrellas held out in front, the three pushed their way through the heavy drizzle to battle against the receding wind.

Chapter Five
Coffee Shop

The three were glad to reach the coffee shop and Beth held the door open as Grace and Mollie climbed the six wooden steps to enter the warmth and light of the inside of this century old wooden building, leaving a wet pathway behind. Alison, the owner had boarded up the ancient windows to protect them from the storm and now she was waiting to welcome her customers with the smell of freshly ground coffee beans and her very own newly baked cakes. Small round tables draped with green and white checked table clothes were dotted around a horseshoe-shaped centre counter, where a few youngsters already sat on tall wooden stools.

Beth spotted a table in the far corner and headed for it, a place where three could sit and relax, away from the crowds. Only now they all had the same idea and were pushing their way in too. Soon the coffee shop was a crush of chattering people and a few whimpering children.

People who had been in fear for their lives now started to arrive with smiles of relief as they found their seats. Everyone felt warm, dry and safe at last as Alison was overwhelmed with orders and shouted back to Becky who worked the coffee machine behind the counter, to hurry up with the drink making.

"I need some help over here!" Becky responded.

She sounded harassed as she complained quietly to herself and a young lad sitting on a stool at the bar heard her and leapt round to help.

"Thanks, Joe," Becky said and smiled at the boy, who was a regular customer.

The three women sat back in their chairs, shook three red umbrellas and laughed. Not only were they removing raincoats with red checked linings but they also carried an umbrella exactly the same and had shaken those waterproof domes all at the same time. Only Beth wore fancy deep pink boots and she wiggled her feet, now poking out from under the table to show the other two and all three laughed, as she, the youngest had been the most sensible one while the other two suffered pairs of sodden feet. Grace's very expensive leather shoes hadn't liked the wet, they were heavily marked and she knew she would have to visit her favourite designer shop to replace them, the next time she was in London.

The new found friends ordered two cappuccinos and one skinny latte, for Grace of course.

What a day, and as they drank their hot steaming coffees they were thankful for the electric lights which still shone and hadn't gone down along with the trees on the edge of the city. Those trees which had stood for hundreds of years were now flattened like matchsticks and would cause a problem for many people on their return journeys.

The three started to chat with each other, spilling out what they had been doing before the storm struck. The sudden realisation that they were safe, released their English reserve and they chatted on about how complicated their love lives were, often saying more than they perhaps should have. They found themselves relaxed in each other's company, even though they were all of different ages and came from different backgrounds. A link had been made and secrets shared, all because of a storm.

***

To gain the attention of the coffee drinkers, someone was tapping a glass mug with a spoon.

"Quiet! Let the man speak," Alison shouted at the top of her voice as she moved her head sharply around, making a few strands of hair drift free from the scooped up, white bun planted on top of her head.

With the chatting of voices and the clinking of glass and china cups coming to a stop, a man's voice was heard. Mollie looked up in great surprise; she knew that voice - Michael.

"It has just come over the radio that the danger has passed, the rain is easing and the wind is dying down. Unfortunately, some roads are blocked and buses are no longer running but it is safe to go outside again."

"Where did he come from?" Mollie whispered as she now lowered her head and her hair fell forward, half covering her round face.

Unbeknown to her, Michael had run from his smashed car into the coffee shop for shelter earlier on and had sat himself close beside a radio.

"Do you know him?" Grace asked.

"He works in my office," Mollie whispered, without lifting her head.

"Well, he's coming over. He looks rather handsome; was he the man you were telling us about?"

"Oh, no," she whispered and dipped her head even lower to try to avoid making eye contact.

"Hi Mollie, would you like a lift back to work?"

Mollie had to look up and their eyes met, she flushed a little and could say nothing.

"The office sent a car out for me, as mine was rather messed up," Michael explained.

Beth, being so young, sometimes didn't think before she acted and pushed Mollie to answer.

"Go on, he fancies you," she whispered in Mollie's ear as she brushed her hair back to show off a huge gold hooped earring.

Mollie hadn't mentioned to these women his married status, otherwise Beth may have been more careful as to what she said.

"I have my own car," Mollie replied at last.

"But the car park is shut. Fallen trees and flood water," Michael said.

"Oh."

Mollie could not find another reason to turn down his offer. All three women finished their coffees as he stood and waited.

Grace and Beth said their goodbyes and set off in their different directions, not thinking they would ever meet again, and hadn't felt the need to swap phone numbers. Michael held Mollie's raincoat and she slipped her arms in. What a gentleman she thought; if only he was free.

***

Grace hailed a taxi which was able to take her back to the airport to look for Josh. She just had to ask him about the red velvet box. Beth ran off in a rush to get home, to check her mother was safe and to sort things out with her. Their relationship couldn't go on the way it was. She started tapping her phone at the same time as she ran, hopping over fallen branches; she was still trying desperately to reach Andy.

Mollie walked quietly at Michael's side, smelling his aroma which was of some kind of expensive aftershave. She liked it but couldn't name it and took another discreet sniff before checking out what he was wearing today. As always, even in a hurricane he looked well dressed and wonderfully handsome as he buttoned up his dark blue suit jacket. Her glance took in his pink shirt and patterned tie as he tucked it inside the jacket. A little young for his age she thought but he could carry it off; he was definitely a very smart man. In fact, the women in the office had commented to each other, he was too smart in his many different expensive outfits to only be paid an office manager's salary.

Mollie didn't want to look into his sparkling green eyes and consequently kept her own blue ones lowered and noticed his tan leather shoes. They looked Italian, definitely expensive and now ruined by the rain.

The chauffeur tipped his cap, held the door open for both Mollie and Michael to enter the back and settle into the deep cream leather seats before he carefully closed the door behind them.

"Thank you Dylan," Michael said with a smile.

Sitting close to Michael, Mollie was unsure of her feelings, yet she wanted him to reach out and hold her hand that lay at her side close by his leg. She must not let him into her heart and she quickly removed her hand to her lap. He noticed her action, felt she was uneasy in his presence. Mollie knew he was not free; Victoria had told her so.

Mollie tried to distract herself by checking out the gadgets and drinks in the back of the rather smart limousine. She enjoyed this opportunity to ride in such a car and rather like an inquisitive child she wondered at her experience before questioning in her mind why a car like this, with a driver, should be sent out to pick up an office manager. But before she could ask such a question they arrived back at the company building's front doors. She didn't notice the sweet smile he wore when watching her check out the car or when he offered his hand to help her out, an offer she took and wished she hadn't when she felt the warmth of his soft skin and her heart jumped.

The chauffeur felt the strained atmosphere within the car but had long since learned not to comment, and as the pair left the car he again tipped his cap and said 'see you again, Sir and Miss'. Michael nodded to Dylan and walked into the building with Mollie at his side.

Chloe, who had returned on a later flight than Mollie the previous day, now stood staring out from one of the windows higher up the building. She'd been watching the storm and soon caught sight of the pair walking in together.

"Hey, girls, look who Mollie's with."

Victoria stood and marched over to the window too. After one look at the couple, she took her frustration out on the girls, telling them to get back to work immediately before she marched off to greet Michael downstairs.

Chapter Six
Grace and Josh

A rainbow appeared over the airport as Grace headed towards it and she wondered if it was a sign.

'*Oh no, I'm getting like that woman, Mollie; she talked on about signs and destiny.*'

Peering from the window of her taxi, she was amazed at the devastation to the airfield. It must have taken a direct hit. The driver had had no problem getting Grace from the shops to the airport but here they saw light aircraft flipped over onto their sides. Sirens were heard blaring from buildings and vehicles alike, golden yellows, reds and blue lights seemed to be flashing in all directions.

Now she was getting worried about Josh. She found herself taking in many short breaths; she could hear her heart beating. It felt as though it would burst from her chest. Suddenly she was aware of that something inside. Was it worry for Josh, who may be injured or worse? Or was it guilt for wanting a better job in her life and for thinking of leaving him, or was this feeling love?

She touched with one hand her throat as she tried to swallow. This sensation started in her middle as if butterflies were fluttering up. She hadn't felt like this before and it scared her.

Straight after leaving school, she and Josh met on the steps of that building as they began their different careers, but it had only been the last few years that they dated and had only recently started living together, which their parents were thrilled about, although they had wished for a marriage. Was it the parents who pushed the youngsters together? Grace thought recently it had been. She felt very confused; surely this relationship was more than just two people drifting along.

The taxi drew up to departures, where there were very few people about. A baggage handler was picking up cases from the roadside and placing them on a trolly alongside a little girl with a woman, and there were a couple of pilots standing on the corner talking.

Grace hopped out of the taxi, paid the driver, telling him to 'keep the change.' She dashed to the automatic doors, wishing they would open faster and still she hung onto her bag with the new dress inside.

She stopped on entering the terminal, turned her head left and right but where to look for Josh? She had no idea, she tried his mobile phone again, still no answer.

The monitor screens now only displayed three words: 'all flights cancelled.'

"He has to be here, somewhere," she spoke out loud, as though he might hear her.

Josh didn't hear her words but could see her from his position on the balcony.

"Grace, up here," a voice bellowed from the floor above.

Josh had been watching the doors, hoping someone would come and help him.

Grace gave a sigh of relief on hearing his voice until she noticed he was bent over the metal railings, as though in pain.

"Josh, are you ok? Stay there I'm coming up," she shouted.

Her heart missed a beat as she ran to the stairs. What was wrong with her? Normally she managed her life, was a calm person, but not here, not now.

"No!" he shouted down.

Grace chased up the stairs, two steps at a time, which was hard in her tight skirt, now riding up her thighs and on reaching the top step she almost tripped forward. She ran to Josh and went to throw her arms around him and kiss him full on his lips but she stopped as her hand felt the wet and cold liquid on his side.

"Oh, you're hurt," she screamed and grabbed his hand to see where the blood was coming from.

Her hand was covered in blood and slipped from his side, which was drenched in red, and as she removed his hand to look, blood spurted out at her, just missing her shopping bag. Josh replaced his hand to the wound and moaned slightly as Grace sat him down and joined him.

There appeared to be no one else around as Grace searched with her damp misty eyes for help, then suddenly a man seized her with his two strong hairy arms, pulling her to her feet. He had crept up from behind her.

"What are you doing? Let me go!" She yelled out in shock.

Grace kicked out with her feet, trying to escape by striking back at his shin bones. She screamed again, even louder this time, but no one other than Josh was there to hear.

"Stay still," Josh pleaded with her.

This prisoner who Josh was going to escort to Scotland had made a run for it during the confusion of scared people making their way to safety when the storm hit. With a knife grabbed from a table in one of the many cafes, he had stabbed Josh as he tried to apprehend him.

Blood was streaming through Josh's fingers now and Grace could see the knife still protruding from just below his rib cage. He was feeling very weak and light-headed; he swayed a little before getting himself upright again.

"I have to help him," Grace pleaded with the man, who still crushed her tightly to his huge sweating body. His odour made Grace feel sick.

"Bill, let her go," Josh faintly demanded.

Bill released Grace, knowing she was no threat to him and she quickly returned to Josh as Bill moved to stand over both with a fork in his hand and now pointing close to Grace's neck.

Grace ignored him and took her lovely new dress from its bag and rolled it into a tight ball, before pushing it under Josh's fingers and around the knife.

"Don't pull it out," she cried at Josh when he touched his side. "Help will soon be here."

Grace looked lovingly at Josh, as Bill snapped at her.

"Come here, woman."

"But I can't leave Josh."

She twisted her head to stare in the face of this dreadful man who had hurt her Josh.

"You will or I will finish him off right here and now. I've nothing to lose. I've killed before."

And Grace noticed a handcuff joined to a short chain hanging from one wrist; she didn't like to think where the other half was.

Grace stood and looked down at Josh with tears stinging at the backs of her eyes, as Bill pulled her aside.

"I'll phone for help," Grace whispered to Josh.

"You won't," Bill shouted back at Grace, and pulled at her arm, making her wobble in her high-heeled shoes. He took no notice of Josh's condition.

Josh tried to give a reassuring smile to Grace but his eyes felt heavy and he found it hard to focus, he was losing consciousness as he slipped sideways.

Struggling, Grace went with Bill to the top of the stairs. She wondered where everyone was as once again she scanned the area for help.

But of course, what had she been thinking, people here would also have been moved to a safe place. Shop assistants had locked up their premises, coffee areas and all bars were deserted, it was like a ghost town and Grace was scared.

Half falling down a couple of steps in those shoes, Grace soon kicked them off, she knew they were not made for dashing about, rather her feet hurt then fall and break a bone. It wasn't long before she found herself outside and being dragged by her arm across the wet tarmac of the short stay car park. Bill was trying door handles as he pushed through the rows of cars; he was going to steal one, which wasn't as easy as in years gone by, when he first turned to crime. But some silly person had dashed from their car in fright, leaving keys hanging from the ignition.

"Yes!" he shouted with glee and grinned at Grace, so very pleased with himself.

Grace continued to plead with Bill to let her phone for help for Josh; she didn't want to lose him now. Suddenly she knew she loved him and she wanted the chance to tell him.

The old rusty red Ford Fiesta would serve Bill's purpose. It was small and quick, easy to drive in and out of places. He shoved Grace into the driver's seat and then decided he would drive after all and pushed her over the gear stick into the passenger seat. She caught her leg on the stick and cried out in pain.

Bill turned the key, checked the petrol gauge, almost full, he noted. He locked the doors. In his mind, Grace was not escaping, she was now his hostage not his driver as he first thought; no he was in charge. Grace rubbed at her leg and looked at her painful, muddy feet. Her tights were torn to shreds, her feet grazed and her raincoat had a button torn off; leaving a ragged hole in the material but that was the least of her worries.

"Where are we going?" Grace asked Bill, trying to keep calm, thinking he wouldn't hurt her if she played along.

"Shut up, woman," he shouted.

He drove off at speed, leaving black tyre marks burned into the tarmac and smelly blue smoke from the rubber curled in the air behind the car. The windscreen wipers were on the highest speed too, splashing back the heavy rain which had returned. Grace quickly pulled her seatbelt across her chest and clicked it into place.

A pair of metal gates were looming as Bill rammed his heavy foot down on the throttle, he was heading at great speed straight for those gates. Grace crossed her arms and brought them up to cover her face, they were going to crash, she was sure of it, she dared not look. Would she die before she told Josh she loved him? Things were flashing through her mind and now she realised she hadn't told him. She was always waiting for him to say those three little words to her.

I love you.

Suddenly a hefty jolt traveled through her body. Grace opened her eyes just as sounds of metal smashing against metal hurt her ears. They crashed through the gates which hadn't been locked and had easily swung open with the impact of the car. She was still alive.

The battered car with its twisted bonnet and the cracked windscreen was speeding down a country lane, around bends far too fast. Grace screamed at Bill to slow down as she hung on tight to her seat. He pulled down hard on the steering wheel while taking another bend. The wheels were screeching as Bill turned to grin at Grace, so smug was he, even though his brow was sweating droplets of water.

Suddenly there was another almighty bang. Bill hadn't seen the tree trunk lying across the road.

The last thing Grace heard was Bill laughing and then she passed out.

Chapter Seven
Beth and Andy

Beth stopped running and walked for ages in the drizzle, head down behind her red umbrella, watching her every step as large branches and twigs hampered her way. How she wished she hadn't argued with her mother that morning and wondered if she was safe in the house alone. Maybe the roof had blown off with that intense wind. She wondered too, was Andy safe and where had he been when the storm hit?

He worked as a salesman for a sweet and chocolate company and spent most of his time on the road, traveling from place to place. A tree could have come down in front of him or, worse still, on top of him, or he could have been blown off the road and left to die somewhere in a water filled muddy ditch. Beth was frightening herself with her vivid imagination. She loved both her mother and Andy, although she didn't like her mother much at the moment; still, she worried.

Sirens sounded in the distance; someone was hurt, going to the hospital in an ambulance. Beth hoped it wasn't anyone she knew, like Andy or her mother, and hoped the person inside was not badly injured.

A dog was barking between its yelping and as Beth passed by a factory fence she stopped to see the poor animal with its leg trapped by part of that wooden fence which had fallen.

"Hello boy, what's happened to you?"

Beth loved animals and squatted down to the dog's level to look into its sad brown eyes.

"Oh dear, got your paw stuck in a hole, have you?" she said.

She lifted the few slats of wood along with its wooden post.

"Come on boy, we will soon have you free," and she ruffled the ears of a black Labrador while talking calmly to him.

Beth threw the wood to one side, took hold of the dog's leg and gently ran her fingers over it, checking that nothing was broken. Replacing the leg carefully to the ground the dog shot off in terror, away from its rescuer.

"Well, thanks, dog, you could have stayed with me," Beth said sarcastically to herself as she watched him run away.

The dog hadn't run far before it stopped, turned around to look at Beth and barked. She called to him and watched as he ran back to stand beside her. She rubbed his smooth shiny coat as he cocked his head to one side. She patted him and looked for a tag on his collar, a tag which might give her a name.

Barney and a mobile number were engraved on a silver disc.

"So you're not a stray then?"

Beth noticed he looked well fed, his coat was in good condition and she somehow felt he came from a good family. But she would have to try the number later, as still there was no signal to her mobile phone.

She pulled the belt from her raincoat and slipped it through the dog's collar to make a lead.

"Come on Barney," she called to him. "You can keep me company on my way home."

The pair walked side by side, Beth thinking she would have loved a dog like Barney to take for walks and play ball with in the park, but her mother often said they couldn't afford one after her father left them. She couldn't remember her father; she was only two when he went and her mother hadn't remarried or taken in a partner. Beth still envied her friends and wished she had had a father to do things with, although she wasn't sure what those things would have been. She wasn't told the real reasons for his leaving. Her mother wouldn't discuss the subject; would she ever?

The sky was clearing, the rain ceased and the wind had dropped. Beth put her umbrella down but didn't roll it up as she quickened her pace to reach the dual carriageway which looped around the city. A few cars were motoring along, only much slower than usual and then she recognised Andy's car. She stopped and waved madly with her flapping red umbrella while also hanging onto Barney's lead. After all, she didn't want him hurt after saving him once that day.

Andy couldn't just stop but he did slow down to gesture to Beth to make her way to the slip road further along.

She was very excited to think Andy loved her so much that he actually came out to search for her, and she ran along the wide grass verge with Barney trotting at her side. Andy waited for Beth to arrive and used this time to inspect his shiny sky blue car. He was thankful that there had been no damage from all those flying objects whipped up earlier by the storm. He loved his new car like so many other men he knew. If he and his mates were not talking about football it was cars.

On meeting, they both threw out their arms to greet and embrace each other. Holding their bodies close, they felt the warmth pass from one to the other as their lips met, they kissed under the red umbrella, a long lingering kiss. Beth had dreamed of that moment often and would grab a kiss whenever and wherever she could; she was hopelessly in love with Andy. Coming up for air and laughing with each other, their embrace fell into lovers holding hands. Their laugh was born from relief that both were safe and Barney sat with his wet shiny nose pointing up at the pair; his eyes appeared to be smiling as he barked for attention. He seemed happy too and when Beth turned to look down at him, he jumped up, landing his two wet paws on her chest.

"Get down," she laughed.

Barney left muddy paw marks on her new raincoat, which meant she could not return it to the shop, but she didn't care anymore.

"You're OK," Beth said and hugged Andy once more. She was looking for another kiss.

"Of course I am." He was six years her senior and sometimes acted out as her protector. That was another reason Beth's mother was against the couple seeing each other; it was her job to protect her daughter.

Her mother's distrust of Andy started soon after Beth enjoyed her 15th birthday. Lisa's friends had passed her information about this young man who was seeing her daughter and she was angry with Beth for keeping quiet about him and of course blamed Andy. Lisa had suffered from a bad experience with Beth's father when she was very young and didn't want her young daughter wasting her life on a man. Lisa felt she had wasted her young life, missed her opportunity to succeed with having a baby to raise.

Andy opened his car door and Barney automatically sprang in, wet coat and dirty paws too.

"Where did the dog come from?" Andy asked, not concerned about the mess he was making when shaking his wet body over the seats.

"I'll tell you on the way home," Beth replied and followed Barney into the BMW.

Andy knew once he took her home he would have to leave Beth at the end of the path because her mother, Mrs Fox, had told him more than once she was having none of his sorts seeing her daughter.

"Flash git," had been another comment thrown at Beth one day when Lisa saw him dropping her off. "Him and that fast car. Who does he think he is, Lewis Hamilton?"

But Beth had been seeing Andy for almost five years now and that was another problem for her mother, because she thought the relationship would have fizzled out long ago. Surely he would have moved onto an older woman of class and with money, what with him coming from a well off family, compared to them: Lisa's low esteem was not always hidden from the world.

Beth was coming to the end of her school years and was determined to finish with good results, to make the grade to enroll and train as a nurse, but she still hoped to marry Andy one day. Not that she ever told anyone this, especially Andy; she didn't want to frighten him off, after his comments on marriage when his friend married, the one who called him a cradle snatcher. Andy remarked on more than one occasion that it was old-fashioned to get married. After all, it was only a piece of paper and a lot of money spent on other people's enjoyment; he would rather buy a house with his money or invest it.

He could be so boringly sensible sometimes, Beth often thought, but still, she loved him.

"You will marry that boy over my dead body!" Lisa screamed one day when arguing with her daughter. But Beth had no idea why she should say such a thing.

In the early days of their relationship, Lisa plotted on how to persuade Beth to leave Andy, although she did consider the fact that he came from a very good family living on the other side of the city, where all the large houses stood. His parents worked hard, it had been said amongst her friends, what was her problem? Beth often asked her mother that very question but didn't get a sensible answer. Andy also held down a reasonable job with good prospects for his future and Beth knew he saved his money but more importantly she loved him.

Anyway, Andy hadn't asked her to marry him. Well not yet.

Chapter Eight
Mollie and ?

Before driving Mollie home from the coffee shop, Michael returned with her to their place of work, to check there were no injuries to staff or damage to the building.

Victoria made sure she met Michael at the building's front doors. She wanted to be first to give her report to him.

"Everything's intact, Michael," she said from those tight red lips. Her narrow eyes spoke a thousand words and none would have been complimentary as she tossed her head away from Mollie. "Each department has been inspected and the chief told me to relay to all the staff to go home to their own properties, in case they have any damage."

"Thank you, Victoria," Michael said, noticing the cold look she threw at Mollie.

Michael decided to leave any issues the two women might have to them. Later he might ask Mollie during her supervision if there was a problem he could help with. He enjoyed supervision time with her to sit and talk. He also knew, only too well, from past experience, that not all women work well together, or men come to that. He remembered the fight between two men in which he had intervened while working in the New York office and the bloodied nose he received for his trouble. He touched his nose in an automatic reaction and recalled it was him who was laid out in one hit on that occasion. This was another reason why he worked out at the gym each week, not that retaliation was ever a good option at work, he knew that.

Mollie made her way to her office area to meet up with Chloe, who was very interested in finding out why she walked in with Michael.

"Come on, tell all," Chloe was questioning Mollie as she arrived back at her desk.

The rest of the team on the fourth-floor were also interested and stopped work to listen to Mollie's explanation. She was unaware that she had been watched from above by her work colleague.

"There's nothing to tell."

Mollie sat to finish her reports for the day. She leaned forward, resting her chin in her hands and dreamed about how handsome and kind Michael was. If only… and she breathed in deeply, trying to recapture his manly smell.

Was she falling in love with a man she couldn't have?

Soon everyone was heading off home and Mollie accepted the offer of another lift.

***

Mollie's mother, Margaret, who had heard a car pull up, stood peering from behind the net curtains. On seeing such a posh car pull up she watched. A man opened the car door for the lady getting out; it was Mollie. Margaret wondered at who might be bringing her home.

"Don't tell me she's actually found herself a man, at last," Margaret said out loud to herself.

The dark green front door opened but only Mollie walked into the hall. Margaret looked around Mollie.

"Well, where is he? I saw him open the car door for you. Looks like a real gentleman to me, is he rich?"

"Mother," Mollie reacted sharply. "He's only our new office manager."

"So, tell me more." A sparkle shone brightly from her mother's eyes. Margaret wasn't giving up hope just yet, even though he only held that position in an office of little size. Anybody was better than nobody, these days.

Mollie wouldn't tell her mother, that as far as she knew he was married and to a man. Her mother wasn't so open-minded in such things as her generation; it wasn't Margaret's fault, she'd been brought up in a different world. With a father who read and lectured from the Bible to his children every day, she was often scared into behaving in a certain way, or she would go to 'Hell', as he had said. Margaret often told Mollie she could still hear her father's voice in her head, even now after so many years.

As Mollie went to her room, Margaret shrugged and returned to her knitting. She ran her own craft business from a small shop on the edge of the city and it was thriving now the fashion was once again for knitted things. Cross-stitch was another pastime for some women but not for Mollie.

Patch, her black and white cat, jumped up and curled around on Margaret's lap, purring as she used her front paws to knead Margaret's legs, like one would, when kneading bread.

"Patch you're leaving fur in my wool," Margaret said as she softly stroked her ears and saw the white patch behind one. She smiled; Margaret loved that old cat and couldn't be cross with her for long. But she did despair of ever seeing her daughter marry and shrugged yet again, and sighed.

"I'm off now mum, see you about midnight." She was on her way to her volunteer work.

"Bye, dear."

"Bye, mum."

Margaret felt she couldn't say any more to a daughter who wouldn't listen. She mumbled quietly under her breath as her only daughter left their home in her car as Mollie's was still stranded in the car park.

"Why can't you meet a nice rich doctor?"

"I heard that," Mollie called back as she slammed the front door behind her, leaving the huge old rusty door knocker rattling as she ran down the footpath, passed the border of roses and daisies her father had set, now knocked about by that wind. Unfortunately, some plants were snapped in two. What a shame; dad would have been so upset to see his flower border damaged. She remembered his smile when he planted them and a tear fell from the corner of her eye.

Standing by her mother's car, Mollie stopped for a moment, held the door handle and looked back at the house, trying to let her mother's words float away.

Oh for goodness sake mother, she thought, remembering Paul, the man who broke her heart several years before. He was a doctor. Paul took that job in London. Mollie had loved him with all her heart but let him go. She sat in the car and remembered how she had pushed him on to succeed in his career as a surgeon. If only she was a selfish woman, she could have had him stay, as he had offered, as a doctor in their local hospital, but she knew he could do better and encouraged him to progress.

He told her he couldn't promise marriage or children while he studied. He had left thinking she didn't really care enough, when really it was he who wasn't ready for commitment.

It took her months, no years, to get over him; that's if she ever had.

Another tear came to her eye as she thought, *he could at least have written.* She laid her head on her crossed arms over the steering wheel, more tears worked their way from the corners of both eyes now and ran down flushed cheeks.

She sat up, thinking she must pull herself together. She started the car's engine. The radio came on, playing a sad song and again she brushed more tears away as she selected first gear and moved away to drive to the hospital. Leaving the housing estate behind with her mother and her remarks, she drove to the very place where Paul had once worked.

***

The team leader of the volunteers at the hospital had phoned Mollie's house. Her mother took the message; a request that Mollie went in to assist nurses attending to people arriving with minor injuries. Mollie worked a few hours a month as a family liaison officer to any youngsters who came in with a drug or drink related problem. Having completed her training last year she enjoyed her role and knew many of the staff and also the layout of the building which could be useful. Being a first aider at her day job would also help with the chaos now mounting in A and E.

Driving along the dual carriageway she passed two young lovers entwined in each other's arms. How she wished it was her in someone's arms, to feel warm and loved and once again her throat felt tight.

Looking in her rear-view mirror, Mollie asked herself if she knew that girl. She thought she did, yes, she recognised the raincoat and the red umbrella, half hiding their embrace. It was Beth and that must be Andy, she thought.

Mollie drove on past the small airport surrounded by a high metal fence, still trying to forget Paul. Suddenly she hit her brakes hard, they screeched as they locked up and her car skidded to a standstill. A tree had fallen across the road. Worse still another car had already hit this tree and steam was pouring from the engine; or was it smoke?

Mollie jumped from her car, her feet splashing into huge muddy puddles, but she took no notice of her water-filled shoes as she ran to help the people inside the car. She placed her hand through the smashed side window, catching her wrist on the jagged glass.

"Ouch," she said as blood appeared and trickled down her hand. She turned off the ignition. That hadn't been an easy task, as a man was half hanging through the windscreen, his rather large body lying over the steering wheel and the keys. He hadn't been wearing a seat belt, Mollie guessed, and then she gasped with shock when seeing Grace slumped next to him. Surely that wasn't Josh with her.

Grace moaned. She was alive.

"Grace, Grace," Mollie called to her.

Grace's eyes, half opened.

"Josh," she murmured and her eyes closed once more.

So it was Josh, Mollie thought and was surprised to think Grace would be with a man so old and unshaven and wearing a prisoner's outfit. Mollie remembered their conversation in the coffee shop. Josh was supposed to be a police officer; had Grace lied to her and Beth?

"No, it's me, Mollie, from the coffee shop, do you remember me?" She shouted, hoping Grace could hear her.

But Grace was drifting in and out of consciousness and only whimpered.

An airport ambulance arrived; blue lights flashing, sirens screaming. The driver had been touring the airport and its perimeter looking for any casualties from the storm. He was expecting to find people trapped in any one of the light aircraft, which landed shortly before the airport was hit, not two people in a car.

Mollie shouted and waved madly at the handsome man running towards her in his paramedic uniform, his medic's bags swinging from his hands.

"Oh, am I pleased to see you," Mollie shouted.

Dropping his extra large medical bag at Mollie's side, he dashed to the car with his smaller one before Mollie could hardly blink.

"Haven't I seen you at the hospital?" he asked Mollie who moved closer to see how the woman was doing.

"Yes, I'm on my way there now," she answered.

As he talked to Mollie he was assessing the situation with the woman strapped in her seat. He had already taken in the condition of the man lying halfway through the windscreen. Both were trapped in a smouldering, crushed car but Mollie's only concerns were for Grace.

"We need to get these two out of here; the car is likely to blow," the paramedic calmly said.

"We can't move them, what about their injuries?" Mollie queried, remembering her first aid course.

"We have to or they might burn. What's your name?" the paramedic asked.

"Mollie."

"Do you know these people?"

"That's Grace, I don't know him but his name could be Josh."

"I'm Jack," he said to both Mollie and Grace who was coming to again.

"We have to get you out." All of Jack's attention was now firmly on Grace.

Grace wasn't able to respond and her gashed head fell bleeding to one side, her eyes closing once again.

"Mollie, take Grace's legs once I've released them."

Jack must remove a piece of twisted metal cutting across both her bleeding legs before she could be moved. Grace was in a bad way; a protruding and bloody bone showed through her skin. She might lose that leg.

"Now, Mollie, I will hold her head and shoulders the best I can. We need to move her as far away from this car as possible."

"What about the man?" Mollie asked.

"I think it may be too late for him. Let's get Grace out first."

Mollie looked down at Grace's leg and her stomach heaved when she saw that bone.

A spine-chilling scream came from Grace as she was moved out of the car and laid on the wet grass verge with a neck brace securely in place. Jack didn't hang around, he seemed to move with the speed of light and Mollie was very impressed.

Flames were licking underneath the car now and Jack made a dash back to try and pull the man out. He couldn't leave him just in case he was wrong and the man was still breathing. He knew he would have little success on his own with a man of his weight but he had to try.

"Jack!" Mollie frantically called. "Get away."

Suddenly, white foam was spurting in great lumps like heavy white foam like candy floss all around Jack. It came from a fire engine which was deployed on the airport grounds. Someone in the control tower had seen the situation and sent the engine to help.

The fire was soon extinguished as still more foam floated over the wire fence. A fireman jumped down from his cab and asked Jack if he needed any help.

"No, mate its fine; the police will be here soon and a second ambulance is on its way too."

The fire crew drove off, having noted the time of the incident. They were ready to report back to their station commander as the police arrived to make their investigation.

Jack went with one of the police officers to check the driver but he had been right; the man was dead. The glass from the windscreen had cut right through a vein in his neck.

"Now let's get you to hospital, with Grace," Jack smiled at Mollie and helped her into the back of the ambulance.

"I'm fine to drive myself," she answered.

"No, you're not, you have been involved in an incident; that can have repercussions later and anyway your arm is bleeding."

Jack covered the wound with a pad and bandage and placed her arm in a sling to elevate it and that's when Mollie noticed the blood stain on the cuff of her new raincoat. Oh no, she thought, '*I have just spent money on this*', but there, she was alive to notice and she smiled to herself, the ever-positive person that she was.

With a click of the car key fob pointed at her mother's car it was locked and parked on the side of the road.

Every available person had taken a vehicle to search for the injured, not only on the airport grounds but in and around the city because so many phone lines were down. Outlying country buildings and roads were also checked. Jack's work partner, Alan, arrived with the second ambulance and its crew. He took to the wheel of Jack's ambulance to drive while Jack sat in the back monitoring Grace and smiling at Mollie.

With blue lights flashing and siren blasting, Alan was racing along towards the hospital. The second ambulance crew would take the man left in the car.

I do like a man in uniform, they are somehow always rather good-looking, and Mollie smiled to herself with her thoughts. *A hero to my rescue! Could Jack be her hero?* She wondered, then she suddenly realised what a mess she must look with her drenched hair hanging in tangles about her face. She thought suddenly of her makeup; it must have run too after that pouring rain returned to cover her and Jack as they stood by that crashed car, and she turned her head away from Jack and patted at the mess, as though to tidy it, which was a waste of time and she gave up.

On their arrival at the hospital doors, a doctor was waiting with two nurses, one of whom Mollie knew. Nurse Rosie helped her down from the back of the ambulance and walked with her to a cubicle inside the building; while Grace went with the most senior doctors and nurses to an area full of monitors and equipment to deal with her injuries.

Mollie chatted with Rosie about the day she had had. How she met Grace, firstly in the shop then enjoyed a coffee with her later. While rubbing at her wet hair with a towel, which was passed to her by a porter, she missed seeing the tall fair-haired senior doctor who she should have recognised from years ago.

"You ok?" Rosie asked noticing her pale face.

Mollie was feeling a little shaken up now. How was she going to tell Grace that Josh was dead. That was of course if Grace recovered from her severe injuries and Mollie coughed, thinking she was going to be sick as she remembered that bone coming from Grace's leg and the bloody mess it had made.

Chapter Nine
Hospital

Beth left Andy around the corner from her small mid terrace house. She had asked him to wait for a text, thinking if her mother was still in a bad mood she would want to go out again. They often met at Alison's coffee shop, where she had been earlier that day. It was a place where all the youngsters met and Alison, the owner, knew them all well. She watched over the years so many boys and girls grow and she had greeted them all with a warm 'hello'.

Beth checked on her mother, to find she was unhurt. Lisa gave her daughter a phone message which she took from the hospital a little earlier that day.

"They want you to go in," Lisa said.

"Thanks mum."

Beth ran off to change her wet clothes and find a dry pair of shoes before heading out to find Andy again.

She told her mother she could always find a lift with another health care worker who lived just down the road; it was easier to tell a little white lie than have another argument about Andy.

Jumping into Andy's car, he drove her to the hospital. She was very excited at the thought of working in A and E; in fact, Beth was beaming all over her face and couldn't stop talking about her work and how she loved it. Andy smiled back at her. She still had a lot of growing up to do. She knew little of the world outside of her mother's grip, but those experiences would come with time. Andy knew that from his own growing up and felt a sense of deep love for his innocent girl. He was unaware of all the emotions she dealt with at work and this gave her different life experiences; she was no little girl. He hugged and kissed her goodbye. Any reason to hug and kiss; in fact, the pair were as bad as each other. Young hormones raced, hands wandered and Andy desperately tried to control his, but longed for the day when they could be true lovers. But he would wait until the time was right for her.

He wished her good luck and felt proud of his girl as he watched her walk through the double doors of the hospital and into the turmoil of injured people. Many of the staff knew Beth was capable enough to help in A and E and that gave her confidence to have her happiest day yet. As a part-time healthcare worker, Beth enjoyed her hours after school and on the weekends, in this local hospital. Normally she would have worked up on the wards but today she was needed in A and E. This was the place to be. It hadn't occurred to her that she might see things she couldn't handle. Death she dealt with on the wards, but not raw twisted bodies coming in from the outside world, before a doctor put the person back together, for her to observe and monitor.

But she had spent her life wanting to be a nurse, since the time she was a little girl playing with her dolls, placing bandages around their middles, legs, and arms, pretending to give them pills which in fact were her own sweets and which she would eat later. Dressed in her little uniform of blue and white striped dress, white apron, and frilly white cap, she knew she would be a nurse when she grew up; she was going to make the sick better.

Now, of course, the uniforms of the nurses and doctors she worked with were very different, tops and trousers may be more sensible but not so charismatic as a dress and frilly white cap or a white coat.

Her heart was set on becoming a good nurse once school was finished with. Only her mother over the years instilled in her that she wasn't clever enough to pass all the exams required, what with her falling behind with her written English and spellings. That's when she decided to take extra lessons, to achieve her goal. She knew she was good with people, sensed their needs and with a spell check on a computer she could cope, she was sure of that.

Beth had been struggling with her self-esteem for a long while now and to get this chance to work alongside these professionals would help her to overcome her doubts. She could push herself forward; see how much she could achieve before leaving school.

She felt her confidence was growing. She felt she was doing ok and her mentors agreed.

***

Bounding through the doors of the hospital after waving Andy off, Beth felt a buzz in the air as doctors and nurses went about their business. In the staff room, she changed yet again. Head held high she was out there on the floor and ready for whatever was thrown at her.

"Where do you want me?" she asked the charge nurse.

"Cubicle four; a woman with a gashed arm is coming in," he told her.

Beth made her way over to await the nurse she would be assisting. Her jobs were all the odd ones, fetching and carrying, making beds and cups of tea but she didn't care; she was watching and learning.

A few minutes went by and a sudden rush took over the area. Doors banged open; a trolley was heading in Beth's direction, pushed by a dark-haired paramedic calling out information on the patient's condition to a tall fair haired doctor who walked alongside. Behind that trolley walked a woman holding her arm up, to help stop the flow of blood and a towel was wrapped around her head. A nurse walked with her and directed this woman towards Beth's cubicle where she would take blood pressure and all the other observations she was trained for.

Beth was suddenly frozen to the spot as she looked from the trolley to the woman with her arm in a sling. She knew them both.

Chapter Ten
Another meeting of three

Hardly believing her eyes, Beth looked from the patient on the trolley to Mollie, who walked with Rosie.

"What happened?" Beth whispered to Mollie not wanting others to know she knew anyone there.

Another nurse, Ann, appeared around the curtains of the cubicle to take over from Rosie, who was not allowed to treat a friend or family member.

"I'll take over," Ann said in her stern voice. She knew all the nurses in A and E, hence knowing that the two knew each other but not Beth. Mollie felt a little faint as the shock suddenly hit her and Beth helped her to sit on the bed.

Rosie told Mollie she would return and left to treat more patients coming in.

Once Mollie's wrist was cleaned and dressed Nurse Ann left. Beth stayed on to settle Mollie with a warm cup of tea and then they were able to chat.

"What happened?" Beth asked again.

Mollie didn't really know anything, other than she had driven up to a car accident where Grace sat next to a man who appeared to have died.

"Who was he?" Beth asked.

"I'm not sure. Grace wasn't able to talk."

Mollie wasn't prepared to tell Beth that she thought Grace's boyfriend was an escaped convict and not a police officer.

"She said she was going back to the airport, to find her boyfriend, Josh, that was his name, wasn't it?" Beth reminded Mollie.

"Yes, that's right."

"So why was she in a car, when she left us in a taxi?" Beth asked Mollie the question, a question Mollie couldn't work out herself. Had Grace lied about Josh?

Beth's young inquisitive mind was going to find out from the other staff.

"I didn't know you worked here?" Mollie continued.

It seemed something of a coincidence that they would meet now when both had worked in the building for some time and both were surprised not to have at least passed in the staff restaurant.

The curtains were suddenly pulled back and Nurse Ann reappeared with a white plastic cup of water and a couple of pain relief pills prescribed by the doctor, for Mollie. Nurse Ann checked these with her notes and passed both pills and water to her patient.

"How's she doing?" Rosie asked as she popped her head through the curtains.

"Yes, ok," Nurse Ann said as she left to assist with Grace, the critical patient.

The gap in the curtains was left open a little wider after Nurse Ann glided through and Rosie noticed Mollie straining her neck to look through. She studied the tall fair-haired doctor who walked by.

It couldn't be. She must be seeing things.

"Paul," the name left Mollie's lips by accident. She shook all over and her face went extremely pale.

"Are you all right?" Rosie asked.

"Do you know Doctor McCloud?" Nurse Ann inquired, returning with Mollie's notes which she placed at the bottom of her bed. She had also caught sight of Mollie peering at him.

"Yes, from a long time ago," and Mollie explained, no more than that.

"Really!" Nurse Ann looked surprised. "He came in to help today as he has moved back to the area and takes up his permanent position here next month," Nurse Ann explained as she left once more.

"No!" And with that Mollie fell back on her pillows feeling sick to the pit of her stomach.

"Are you sure you're alright?" Rosie asked again, as she checked her vital signs on the monitor. All read correctly but Rosie asked Beth to go and find a doctor who was free to come and check on Mollie.

"So what's up?" Rosie pushed Mollie to answer her, now Nurse Ann and Beth had both left.

Rosie could be the whole hospital gossip column for the in-house newspaper; she seemed to know everything that went on. All the day to day titbits found their way back to Rosie, yet she wasn't nasty with any of her information, not like *Victoria*.

"We were an item for a long while and I thought we might marry one day," Mollie whispered to her friend Rosie.

"Oh yes, of course, I remember now. Do you want me to pull the curtains together?"

"Yes please."

"I have to leave you for the moment, but I will be back," and Rosie smiled as she left.

As Rosie went to help with Grace, Beth returned with a doctor.

Mollie lowered her eyes and asked Beth if she could get her some more water to drink, she wanted Beth gone.

As Beth left, Doctor Paul McCloud smiled at Mollie and walked closer to her bed and reached out to take her hand.

Chapter Eleven
Love

"Mollie?" Paul asked as he pulled back his hand with a stunned look on his face.

He picked up her notes which lay at the end of her bed. Reading her information, he turned and looked again at this woman. It really was Mollie, the woman he had loved.

"It is you. You've changed your hair."

Paul always noticed her changes even down to what she wore. She thought it was a wonderful thing at the time, but over the years she realised he was aware of anything that changed. After all, he was a doctor and that's what they looked for every day of their lives; changes could mean life or death in his world.

"Hello Paul," Mollie sheepishly said.

"It really is you and you're ok, ready to leave, I see, in an hour or so."

He replaced her notes and this time went to hold her hand. She pulled away, feeling uncomfortable with the man she used to love. Would his touch re-ignite her feelings? Did she want that?

Paul felt awkward too and stepped back from the bed.

"Well, I'm pleased to see you again. I'll pop back before you leave."

Mollie said nothing but watched and remembered as he walked from her bed towards another patient who needed his care. She heard him speak gently to a woman and Mollie reflected on him, Paul McCloud, still the polite, considerate doctor with the bedside manner.

Now, what shall I do? Mollie wondered as she watched Paul at work, this man whom all the staff respected.

Perhaps I can slip away before he returns.

She was afraid of her feelings and settled back on her bed to ponder some more.

I bet he wants to see me again, pick things up where we left off. Now he is a top doctor, he will think I want him, for his position and money. Perhaps he has come back to marry me. Mollie rubbed her head, remembering how she told him everything her mother had said about marrying for money. After all, he said he would come back for her once he was rich and promoted, but that wasn't what Mollie longed for any more. She wanted to hear those three little words *I love you*, just as Grace and Beth had said they wanted to hear, from their men, when discussing love over coffee.

Then it dawned on her, perhaps he was already married, to some highly qualified woman. *Bitch,* and Mollie frowned at her thoughts. *Why am I having nasty thoughts about this man I wanted to marry all those years ago?* Mollie was getting cross with herself now. No, she wanted to find out more about her dashing hero, Jack, she told herself and smiled as she thought she could really like him. She remembered how Jack dashed from his ambulance, his medical bags swinging in his hands, arriving to take charge of the situation. How strong he had been, when pulling Grace out of the car and oh, so very brave, to go back for a man who was clearly dead. *He was her hero at that moment.*

Paul would be a steady calm man to be with and earn far more money than Jack, but what was she thinking? Neither of them had asked her out, let alone talked about marriage and with those silly thoughts, she said out loud: "stop it; I am not desperate."

"Desperate, for what?" Rosie said as she returned.

"Nothing."

"Get yourself ready, Mollie and I'll take you home." Rosie was coming to the end of her shift.

Mollie found her bag and slid down from the bed but still carried on comparing Jack and Paul in her mind; she couldn't help it however much she told herself she wasn't desperate.

How different the two men looked in colouring and body shape. Paul was tall, thin and fair. He wore large rimmed, round glasses, which she thought made him look very intellectual. Jack was tall and dark, with muscles that pulled at his shirt sleeves and she smiled at the thought of seeing his chest uncovered, perhaps dark hair hiding a six pack. He was a man of action, also very well informed in his job but joked a lot. Both men were clever and saved lives and Mollie liked that.

She knew all about Paul, his funny little ways, the food he liked and oh yes, the red wine must be of good quality or he complained it tasted like vinegar, once making quite a scene in a very exclusive restaurant.

Although she wouldn't move in with him on a permanent basis, she had stayed over a few nights after dating him for more than two years, but she knew nothing of Jack. Suddenly she found she wanted to know more about her dashing hero.

Did he like fine wine and good food? Maybe not, more like a curry and a beer she suspected. He wore no wedding ring but that didn't mean he wasn't married. He had smiled and been kind to her but he hadn't asked her out; well of course he hadn't, she was his patient and he treated her the same as anyone else.

Mollie was dressed and ready to leave knowing her life must change, sooner rather than later, and she hadn't given Michael a second thought.

***

Grace was in a bad way and was asking for Josh in her feeble voice during her conscious moments. The staff tried to find the woman's details from her raincoat pockets, but there was nothing there to help. She hadn't a bag with her either, so who was she?

In the meantime, Josh was brought in by another ambulance from the airport and was asking after Grace. He now lay in an area not far from her where he was treated by those highly skilled doctors and nurses while waiting to go to theatre. He had lost a lot of blood and needed to be stabilized before going into surgery and still, he asked after Grace. He tried to explain about her abduction by a prisoner in his charge and how he'd dragged her from the airport lounge.

"Can you phone my girlfriend?" he asked his nurse; her name was Rosie.

"I will try, do you have her number?" Rosie enquired.

By now Josh was getting very distressed and breathless but he managed to answer.

"It's on my phone," and he raised his hand very slowly to point to a clear plastic bag containing his clothes. Rosie felt in his pocket.

Rosie took the phone from the pocket of his trousers. She found the little red velvet box and pulled it from its hiding place.

"What's this, if you don't mind me asking?" Showing Josh the box, a twinkle in her eye came about from a happy thought in her head.

Josh closed his eyes while trying to lift his arm, which was a struggle against the pain. He signalled to Rosie to put it back.

"I'm so sorry, I shouldn't have asked, it's none of my business," and she started to replace the box back in the pocket.

"No, take a look," Josh managed to say.

As she lifted the lid of the red velvet box, the overhead light caught the stone, and it sparkled.

"Oh, it's beautiful," Rosie exclaimed, beaming all over her face. "Gosh. When were you going to ask her?"

Rosie was full of excitement for the lovers and it was another piece of information she could use that no one else knew, something else to gossip about in the staff room.

"I tried asking this morning," and then Josh stopped to take a breath. "I was called away." He took another breath, rested again. Speaking, was getting harder. "It wasn't the time or place for such a question." He hesitated and closed his eyes, before speaking again. "Perhaps she wouldn't want to wear it."

"But why?" Rosie was mystified; surely they must have been together for some time, for him to even buy such a stunning diamond solitaire.

"She has an interview," he explained, hesitating to catch his breath. "Tomorrow in a different city to where I'll be working."

His eyes closed yet again, worn out from just talking.

"Oh, I see," Rosie said as her expression saddened and she shut the box which could hold his future and replaced it in the trouser pocket.

"You won't tell her?" Josh just managed to ask his kind nurse as he drifted off into an unsettled sleep from all the pain relief.

Rosie had a problem with keeping secrets but she would try, and she nodded at Josh before studying his mobile phone. Rosie said no more but pressed Grace's number, the phone sent out a call.

Josh came to. His drifting in and out of sleep was happening more and more and the doctors needed to get him to theatre, quickly.

Rosie and Josh waited for Grace to answer.

***

Jack jumped as a phone went off in his top pocket; it was the phone he had picked up from the well of the red Ford car. He'd forgotten he placed it there.

"Hello," he answered the caller, hesitantly.

"Who's that? I know that voice," Rosie questioned.

"Jack, I'm a paramedic."

"Jack, what are you doing with that phone?"

"Rosie, is that you?" Jack asked.

"Come round to the nurse's station, right now," she demanded.

Rosie was not one to be messed with when at work. She might be a gossip and a laugh but her work she took very seriously.

Walking up to Rosie, Jack was nodding; his face asked his questions as he held up the phone.

"Where did you get that?" Rosie was the first to ask a question.

"From the car accident the man and woman were in. I forgot to pass it over in all the rush, sorry."

Jack knew he could be in trouble if anyone thought he had kept it.

"Well, I have her boyfriend here and he wants to talk to her."

Both Rosie and Jack walked closer to Josh's bed as they talked.

"I'm not sure she is going to make it, the other feller in the car didn't," Jack whispered in Rosie's left ear, half covered by her red curly hair. "Where is she?"

"Through there with Beth. She's keeping watch over her at the moment. She is too ill to go to theatre, but a surgeon is on his way down to help get her stabilised." Rosie kept her voice low and looked away from Josh.

"What's going on?" Josh pleaded with Rosie in his weak voice, while pulling at the blue scrub's covering her rather large hips. She often made fun of her own hips, saying she was short and cuddly. Rosie didn't worry about her size, not like Grace who was tall and slim but now lay next door close to death.

It was often said that Grace, with her pale skin and naturally blonde hair, could have been one of those top models on the front of a magazine, but that was something she didn't want, even though she watched her weight and had a good figure. She kept herself in shape but at this very moment, she lay in a hospital bed bloodied and broken, her skin paler still. Jack rolled his eyes and gave a nod of his head, to tell Rosie she must tell Josh what was going on with Grace, to prepare him for the worst but Rosie would have to clear that information with a doctor first. She turned away from Josh as Jack gently patted Josh's shoulder trying to reassure him.

"I'll go and see what I can find out, mate," Jack said as he turned to leave.

"Where are you going?" Josh pleaded with Rosie, as a porter and nurse came to collect him for theatre.

"I'll tell you as soon as I know, after your operation, ok."

Josh would have to wait until tomorrow for news of Grace.

While Rosie spoke to a doctor, Jack walked passed Mollie's cubicle. Noticing she was ready to leave, he decided to go in for a chat.

"You're looking better," Jack said with his charming voice, followed by one of his biggest smiles. He rather liked this woman but he must be professional while at work. Later he thought, he would find out where she lived.

"Yes, I'm fine; I'll be out of here soon." Mollie smiled back at him, a little happier with her hair looking tidy after a good brush.

"I can arrange for someone to collect your car and drop it at your house, if you like to give me the keys."

"Jack; that would be really helpful, as it's mum's car. Thank you"

And Mollie passed him her keys as well as her address; she thought that would bring about another meeting.

"Is anyone coming to collect you?"

Mollie told him Rosie was taking her home and Jack turned to walk away.

"Don't go. Tell me, how's Grace?"

"I can't say, sorry, confidentiality and all that." And Jack turned to leave once more.

"How about the man left in the car? Was he Josh?" Mollie needed to know.

Jack stopped and turned back, he was unable to reassure Mollie that Grace would pull through, but he could tell her the man wasn't Josh. Jack then left in a hurry to catch up with his partner, Alan, who was waiting to go out on another call.

Mollie worried for the woman she had had coffee with that very morning and knew from their conversation that she wanted to meet up with her boyfriend to discuss their future, before either of them flew out to the possibility of different lives. Grace told both Beth and her about the red velvet box and what she thought was inside and whether she wanted what it represented.

Mollie also wondered if anyone had told Josh of Grace's injuries or her of his.

***

Rosie was coming to the end of her shift, likewise Beth. Both were tired and headed for the coffee machine in the staff room. Collapsing together on the sofa with mugs of coffee in their hands, Beth curled her legs up as Rosie swung around and extended her own short legs onto the next chair.

"What a shift," Rosie said and took a sip of her black coffee.

Beth agreed, quietly smiling to herself. She loved working in A and E and decided there and then she would do everything in her power to become a great nurse, not just a good one.

"I'm off home," Rosie said. "You coming?"

"No, I will wait to see how my friends are doing."

Beth thought of Mollie and Grace as her friends now and then there was Josh, of course; she wanted to know how he came through his operation.

"Well, I'm taking Mollie home."

"Of course, you know her," Beth stated the obvious. "That's fine; I will stay with Grace and Josh."

Beth had grown up massively over that shift and she phoned Andy to say she was staying at the hospital and not to collect her.

Chapter Twelve
The next morning

Beth woke up in the staff room, stiff and aching from the position in a chair where she had lain overnight. Some kind person had placed a hospital blanket over her during those hours.

"Wakey, wakey, your mother's on the phone. She wants to know, where the hell you've been all night. You'd better take the call. She thinks you've been sleeping with the boyfriend."

Sam, the night nurse was just going off duty and Beth could see the cheeky grin on his face as he watched her rub her eyes and try to make sense of where she was. She shook her head in despair of her mother, then sheepishly took the phone from Sam.

"Hello mum," she said quietly while still rubbing her eyes and yawning.

"What are you playing at, my girl? Get yourself home, right now."

"No mum, I'm staying here. I have a friend in a bad way," and with that said, she put the phone down. Beth was surprised at herself for doing such a thing.

"Just how old does she think I am?" Beth complained to herself as she sharply walked over to the coffee machine and hit its buttons.

Beth wouldn't normally be mean to her mother but she was fed up with all her moods and rules. She plonked herself down and drank her half warm coffee, dammed machine was failing again, she thought as she stood and proceeded to walk to the bathroom.

Having splashed water over her face she was ready to make her way to the intensive care unit, to sit by Grace's bed.

Doctor McCloud had been the surgeon who cared for Grace throughout the night and no member of his team thought she would pull through. After a while, Beth decided to check on Josh who was being nursed in a recovery ward on the floor below. He was still sleepy but as he slowly opened his eyes he soon recognised Beth from the night before.

"Grace," was the first word to leave his lips, though it was obviously a struggle for him to talk.

"She's fine, don't you worry," Beth lied; she didn't really know. She hadn't the training to know her condition but at least she knew Grace was clinging on to life. With that little piece of information given, Josh drifted in and out of sleep, brought on by his earlier anesthetic. Beth had satisfied herself that Josh would make a full recovery after talking with the ward sister and she returned to sit with Grace for a while, before facing her mother at home.

"You just have to make a full recovery. Josh loves you, he has a ring for you," Rosie had told her and now Beth whispered in Grace's ear. Whether she heard or not, Beth didn't know.

Beth's mobile phone beeped, a message from Andy, 'you ok? xxx'

Hitting the phone's screen, Beth sent back a reply 'fine c u later, xxx'. She was too tired to write more.

Rosie was the one going to see Josh later that day, to explain the nature of his girlfriend's problems.

As the morning passed by, Beth read a few magazines between keeping a watchful eye on Grace lying in a hospital bed with tubes invading her body; she was very poorly.

Still none of her family had arrived; surely they would be here soon. Beth's mind drifted for a moment. She wished Andy would buy her a ring and if anyone had seen her face they would have known she would say yes the moment he asked the question. But for now, her face looked sad, for only yesterday she sitting with those two women, drinking coffee and laughing together.

Beth thought of their conversation. Mollie had talked about a lost love. What was his name? Paul, Beth suddenly remembered. Mollie also said he was a doctor. Beth recalled the look on Mollie's face and how she reacted in A and E when Doctor Paul McCloud walked by. Was he one and the same?

She, in turn, had talked of Andy to those two women and how focused he was on earning money for their future. Grace had talked about her concerns, with Josh. Looking at Grace now, Beth realised life could change so quickly

All three women felt they could share information with strangers on that day, more easily than they could with family members.

Beth was brought from her thoughts when she heard the quietest of moans.

"Josh?" Grace was coming to.

Beth pressed the buzzer and a nurse came running, she called for a doctor. Beth stood back to watch them work; she was in awe of these people. What a wonderful team. She very much wanted to join them.

"Grace is a fighter. I think she might just make it, but it will be sometime before she leaves this hospital," the doctor remarked.

"Time Beth went home," the morning staff said to each other before telling her. They only had words of praise for all her good work.

Andy came to collect Beth and she fell into his arms and they kissed slowly, affectionately.

"Oh, Andy, so much has happened," she was going to tell him all, once she was in his car, but very soon she was dozing with the car's movement. She was too tired to even say how she enjoyed her shift, even though it was at the expense of other people's suffering, but she knew she had helped to deliver comfort and care and that pleased her. *'Job satisfaction,'* were the words Andy remembered hearing.

Needing her own bed, Beth almost fell through the kitchen door where her mother stood waiting.

"What do you want?" Lisa turned on Andy, who held Beth's arm, supporting her as she walked in. Beth was almost falling asleep in his arms.

"I drove her home, Mrs Fox," he said politely.

"Well, you can go now," Lisa snapped back and took her arm.

She steered her to her bedroom, where Beth collapsed onto her bed to sleep. Covering her with a quilt her mother removed her shoes and lightly kissed her daughter's forehead before whispering, *I love you, sleep well my darling*

Chapter Thirteen
Barney and Beth: A Dog's Love

Some hours later a cold wet nose and rough tongue lapped around Beth's face. She rubbed her hand over her skin as her eyes popped open. She had totally forgotten about Barney, the dog she brought home.

"Hello there, have you been fed?" Beth said as she pulled herself up in her bed to sit and look into Barney's big brown eyes. Barney placed his front paws on the quilt and cocked his head to one side.

"Of course he has; I wouldn't starve the poor creature, now would I?" Her mother arrived with a mug of tea in her hand. "I've phoned the number on the collar and left a message; fancy hiding a dog in your bedroom."

Beth was amazed at her mother who took the time to feed Barney and seemed happy to have a dog in her home. Previously over the years she told Beth she couldn't have a dog.

Beth went for a shower and dressed before going downstairs. As she passed the lounge on her way to the kitchen she saw her mother making a fuss of Barney.

"You're a lovely old dog, aren't you?" she heard her mother say.

Barney looked up into Lisa's face and if a dog could smile he would have been grinning from one of his floppy ears to the other.

Sitting down at the table Beth poured herself a second mug of tea as she watched the news. There were many pictures of the storm damage while remarks were being made by presenters about the weather forecasters. Some complained bitterly about the confusion their information had brought about and how they must be sure of their facts next time, if there was a next time.

The toast popped up and Beth buttered two slices before it went cold. Toast, butter, and marmalade were just entering her mouth as the phone rang.

"Hello," she heard her mother say.

Beth couldn't hear what was being said, but she got the gist of it from her end; it was someone about Barney.

"That's fine, come over later, we will be here."

Her mother walked through to the kitchen with the phone still in her hand.

"Who was that?" Beth asked.

"Some woman about Barney, Miss Redhurst, Mollie, I think she said her first name was."

Beth looked up, startled by the name, it couldn't be? Could it? The Mollie she had met only yesterday? No, surely not.

Lisa decided not to mention the night before and Beth left the subject well alone too. That way she wouldn't have to explain herself. Lisa was too engrossed with Barney anyway. She seemed as though she loved that dog and in such a short space of time. Beth was very surprised but it was lovely to see her mum smiling again.

***

The front doorbell rang and Beth answered it.

"Mollie, it is you. Well, come in; let me take your raincoat."

Beth emphasized the word *raincoat* and both women smiled at each other. The coats had become a talking point in a funny sort of way. The rain would drizzle on for some days after that storm and so the coat was useful, even though Mollie still hadn't cleaned the blood stain from its cuff.

Beth led Mollie through to the lounge where Barney sat close to Lisa's legs; he cocked his head to one side but at first did not move to greet Mollie.

"Barney," Mollie said as she bent down and reached out her hands.

Barney looked up at his new mistress before dashing over to Mollie.

"Hello, boy," Mollie said as she rubbed his back. Barney lapped around her face now.

Lisa was wearing a woeful look, a look Beth couldn't ever remember seeing before.

Tea and cake were offered to Mollie by Beth and the two sat to chat between mouthfuls of cake and cream. Lisa declined cake and wouldn't join in the chatting either. She looked at Barney, who returned to her side and laid his head on her lap.

"He's an old dog now and misses me when I'm at work." Mollie looked at Lisa. "Plus, of course, I'm often out in the evenings and I'm afraid my mother doesn't really like having him around the house since dad went. You know he died recently?"

"I'm so sorry," Beth said and touched Mollie's arm in a sign of sympathy.

"Thanks," Mollie said and smiled.

"Barney keeps running off and that's how he came to be at the factory grounds, where dad had worked. I suppose he was looking for him. We must keep in touch," Mollie added, as she left with Barney on his lead.

"Yes, perhaps we will see each other at the hospital, why don't you come and visit Grace," said Beth. "She'll need company, she's going to be in there a long while."

"I'll do that," Mollie promised as she left for home.

Having stood at the door watching Mollie pull away in her car, Beth turned around to step back and almost fell over her mother.

"I'm going to lie down," Lisa said sharply and left for her bedroom.

Beth noted her mother watched Barney leave and seemed sad at losing him. With only a day together she had fallen in love with that dog and now she put herself to bed in a bad mood. Beth knew to keep her head down when her mother went into one of her moods.

Beth decided on an early night too, as her mother did not reappear. Beth locked up the house, took a dinner from the freezer and placed it in the microwave; that would have to do for tonight's meal. She was tired after the night of lying in a hospital chair. Beth settled down in bed on a full stomach to dream of Andy and actually missed Barney lying at the side of her bed. She thought of her mother and the attention she had given the dog.

***

The sun shone into Beth's bedroom early the next morning and as she woke she heard a whimpering and scratching at the front door. She shot out of bed, drew her pink curtains, looked down from her window to see Barney sitting on the step.

Hurrying down the stairs Beth headed for the door. Picking up the house keys from the small hall table, she fumbled to place them in the lock.

"What's all the noise? Where are you going?" Lisa called after Beth.

"It's Barney, he's back," she shouted up the stairs.

"No!" Lisa said and dashed down still in her pyjamas, feeling excited for the first time in a very long time.

Lisa pushed Beth aside and opened the door; Barney bounded through. Lisa bent down and made a great fuss of him. Beth had hardly shut the door when the phone rang; she answered it. The voice the other end was Mollie's, asking if Barney was there.

"Yes," Beth replied. "Are you coming round?"

About an hour later Mollie arrived but she was on her way to work and couldn't stop for long.

"Could you possibly keep him for the day? He keeps running off since dad died. I think mother has been neglecting him." Mollie asked the question while looking across at Lisa.

"Oh, yes," Lisa's eyes opened wide and shone brightly as she rubbed at Barney's head.

"Are you sure mum? I'm going to the hospital after Andy picks me up."

"Yes dear, its fine, you go."

Not even the mention of Andy's name took the smile from her mother's face.

"That's fantastic; see you at the end of the day."

Mollie left, passing, Andy on the path.

"Well, let the boy in," Lisa said.

"Good morning Mrs Fox," Andy dared to say, as he gingerly stepped a foot inside the house.

Lisa didn't answered Andy, only brushed passed him on her way to the kitchen to find dog biscuits which she had asked a neighbour for only yesterday.

The two youngsters looked at each other amazed at Lisa's reaction. Andy waited quietly by the door for Beth before driving her to the hospital from where he would go on to the sports shop. After hugging and kissing Andy, Beth was still smiling as she walked through the hospital doors.

"See you later," they had both said together.

By the time everyone arrived home that night, Barney would have a comfy bed made up of old blankets of many colours and Lisa would be humming a happy tune and even smiling.

"What's up with your mother?" Andy winked at Beth after dropping her back at home that evening.

"Don't ask; it's Barney's doing," and Beth smiled at her boyfriend who actually got inside Beth's home for the second time that day, which was quite an achievement.

Andy loved Beth; Beth loved Andy and now Lisa loved Barney. A dog which came unexpectedly into their lives and who seemed to have helped her mother back towards her old, kind self and that made Beth happy too.

Chapter Fourteen
Emotional Love

Josh was out of bed and in a wheelchair parked beside Grace's bed.

"Come on Grace, wake up, talk to me," he had whispered many times to her.

Josh didn't hear Beth walking up behind him before she touched his shoulder.

"Good morning," Beth spoke quietly to him.

"Beth?" he said as he turned to see her standing by his side.

"How's Grace?" she asked.

"Doing ok, the Doc said," and Josh smiled which helped take that strained look from his drawn face.

The pair said nothing more for quite a long while until Beth noticed the wall clock.

"Look at the time, I have to go."

She would return later after the extra shift she was working that morning. The school exams had finished for her and she would spend even more time here at the hospital.

Grace only came round the once, while Beth was there to hear her ask for Josh and since then Josh had sat at her bedside waiting. He took his meals there; he told the nurses he couldn't leave her, he must be there when she opened her eyes and he worried that may not happen. He couldn't imagine life without Grace and secretly fingered the red velvet box now placed in his dressing gown pocket.

Later that afternoon Beth popped in to say goodbye to both Josh and Grace before meeting up with Mollie in the hospital restaurant for a chat. Mollie was to start her few hours of support work later that evening.

"Grace is on the mend but still not fully conscious at the moment," Beth told Mollie.

"I will go to see her anyway," Mollie replied. "It's good to talk to someone, they say, whatever condition they are in."

"Her boyfriend has been by her side all day." Beth continued.

"Really? His name is Josh isn't it?"

"Yes, he seems to care a lot for her."

"I've seen the ring you know, it's gorgeous," Rosie said as she came up behind the two women.

Rosie sat herself down and placed a cup of tea on the table. She was ready to join in the conversation about love. All the different types they discussed in the next hour, just as the three women had in the coffee shop that day of the storm.

Men and women, children and parents, grandparents, and even the love between animals and people, love can cross all boundaries, they all agreed.

"Animals," Mollie piped up above the other two. "Beth, would your mother like to keep Barney?"

"What?" Beth hadn't seen that question coming and thought, no way would her mother have a dog permanently in their house.

"Well, I don't know. Don't you want poor Barney anymore?" Beth frowned as she asked.

Mollie remembered how Barney melted her heart when he was a puppy, but it was unfair to leave him all day as both she and Margaret worked and her dad was the one who walked him, played ball with him and he wasn't here now. Mollie felt a lump appear in her throat.

Mollie began to explain that she and her mother had discussed the subject and decided it would be the best for Barney as her mother was none to keen on the dog or her dad come to that. The other two girls looked across at each other in surprise but passed no comment. Mollie didn't noticed their looks, but knew she shouldn't have said that.

"Barney seemed to take to your mother, Beth, and her to him. Please take him." Mollie carried on talking.

"I'll talk to mum when I get back." Beth said.

"I must get to A and E now," Rosie said as she stood and pushed her chair under the table.

"Before you go, who was that man who died in the car?" Mollie asked Rosie.

"An escaped prisoner. See you later," and Rosie was gone.

Beth's phone buzzed on the table, it was Andy. A text, 'where are you, been sat outside ages.'

Mollie noticed Beth's face draw in, her lips go tight and her trimmed eyebrows narrowed as the colour drained from her face.

"What's the matter?" Mollie asked.

Beth grabbed a raincoat from the back of the chair, rammed her phone into its pocket as though she was mad at Andy. She stopped to move her dirty cup to the collection point and her raincoat slipped from the chair to the ground. Mollie picked it up and replaced it on the back of the chair.

"Nothing wrong, is there?" She asked.

Beth grabbed a raincoat without a word and left Mollie sitting at the table. Beth ran off to meet Andy outside. She thought the text a little short, not like her Andy at all, no xxx or love you, why was that? She thought.

When they met, there was no hugging or kissing. Beth couldn't understand what was wrong, what she had done to upset Andy.

Andy shoved his phone under Beth's nose and she saw the photo of herself kissing another man.

"Who sent this?" she shouted back at Andy, her heart in her mouth, her eyes stinging from forming tears. Her legs went weak as she stood by Andy's car.

"You don't seem surprised." Andy was now pointing at this unknown man in the picture, who must have turned forty, he thought. "It doesn't matter, who sent it; he looks years older than me," he bellowed.

"Andy, he's nobody, really, it happened at the hospital Christmas party."

"So you do know him?" Andy was angry to think she had deceived him.

"Who sent this?" Beth asked again.

"Why did you tell this person, you love him and hate me?" Andy stared at Beth with penetrating eyes as he scrolled the picture down to show her those words.

"I didn't," Beth sobbed.

Suddenly Andy was consumed with jealousy and was acting like a teenager instead of a man in his middle twenties. He wasn't ready to listen to reason and turned away from Beth, jumped into his car and roared off, grating the car's gears as he went. She was left standing in the hospital car park with tears streaming down her face. Andy had given her no time to explain. The doctor was unknown to her at that time but now she knew exactly who he was.

"Andy!" she screamed after him as his car disappeared down the road.

Beth walked slowly over to the bus stop with her head hung down, feeling rejected and very miserable as she sat down on that silly little seat that flips up when you stand. Her face was still pale but now with pink cheeks that held black streaks of mascara. Her red eyes were sore and she sniffed her bright pink shiny nose, before giving out a deep breath. She could feel a headache coming on.

How could Andy think she hated him? What was she going to do? She had dreamed of marrying him only last night.

The local green bus pulled up and the rain began again as she ran up the stairs to sit at the top, on her own. She didn't want to bump into anyone she might know. She felt for her phone in her raincoat pocket, but it was not there. She didn't even have a tissue hiding in there.

The bus passed fallen trees, now cut into logs by men who had worked with massive chainsaws. She felt her heart was cut into pieces too and by a man she loved. The tears continued to trickle down her face, as did the rain down the bus windows.

On arriving home Beth ran to her bedroom, stamping up each step of the stairs as though it was its fault she hurt so much. She slammed the door behind her before throwing herself across her bed, where she sobbed into her pillows.

She didn't expect her mother to come and find her, ask her if she was all right. She hadn't before, if she thought it may involve Andy. How wrong can a teenager be? For there stood her mother on the other side of her door knocking gently and asking what was wrong and if she could come in.

Beth argued with herself as to letting her mother in. Should she tell her what Andy had done to her? Her mother would only say, I told you so.

Lisa opened the door slowly and poked her head around it to see her distressed daughter lying across her bed. Beth was aware of her mother standing by her side but didn't move to acknowledge her.

Lisa sat on the edge of the bed and laid a hand gently on Beth's shoulder.

"Mum, he dumped me," she sobbed.

Lisa said nothing, what could she say? After all these years she knew Beth was an independent happy girl who had a mind of her own and would do what she wanted to do. Lisa was just beginning to see that Andy wasn't so bad. He stuck around and until now hadn't made her daughter cry.

"But why?" she asked.

"That stupid drunken man at the Christmas party. He grabbed a kiss from me, before laughing with his mates. What could I have done mum?" Beth wept into her hands as she pulled herself up to sit by her mother.

"Come on, I'm sure its all a big misunderstanding." Lisa tried to console Beth before asking how Andy found out.

Beth explained about the picture on his phone as her phone bleeped in her raincoat, only it was Mollie who pulled the phone from the pocket.

***

Mollie left the hospital in a raincoat she struggled to get on. The sleeves felt tight and were rather shorter than before, the buttons hardly met at the front. That's strange, she thought, it shouldn't have shrunk and I'm sure I haven't put that much weight on so quickly. Mollie was often on a diet which may only last a couple of days, she enjoyed her food too much to ever lose weight but she kept it constant

The clouds started to sprinkle light rain again. She tried to pull on the raincoat but it was tight around her middle. A phone bleeped in the pocket. She felt for it and pulled out a phone which didn't belong to her.

A picture of a man wearing a silly Christmas hat and kissing Beth was displayed on its screen. Mollie was shocked, she knew that man's face, it was Paul. She scrolled down to read the words under the picture. *'Andy, Beth loves me.'*

Mollie's hand trembled. How could he? Beth was barely nineteen, he was almost forty. Andy had posted that picture to Beth's phone, adding his own words: 'it's all over between us.'

Mollie felt Beth's pain. She would have to go and see her tomorrow and find out the truth. Mollie now understood why Beth had gone so pale and left in such a hurry and she decided there and then that she was going to sort this mess out.

Chapter Fifteen
A week away

Mollie tried phoning Beth on her land line, had even been around to her house but no one answered. The woman next door said they had gone away.

A week past and the world for three women who met in a shop had dramatically changed. Mollie was thinking the storm brought bad vibes with it. It had uprooted trees and now it seemed to have pulled people's lives apart too. Beth had said something similar to Lisa.

"Don't talk such rubbish," Beth's mother told her, over yet another breakfast, where she moped and ate little. Beth made up stuff in her head which she then voiced to her mother. "That boy has a lot to answer for," Lisa stated, as she stroked Barney's head under the table.

The bed and breakfast lady asked how long they might be staying.

"We thought, perhaps we would leave tomorrow, if thats ok?"

"Fine. I just wondered," and she left to serve tea at the next table. She had been quite happy to accommodate a dog and Barney enjoyed his walks on the sandy beaches while mother and daughter talked.

Lisa decided to take Beth away, so she could sort her head out.

During those days away when Beth was feeling unsettled without Andy, her mother opened up about her younger life, explaining a little of how she had met her father. About their brief marriage and how young they had been, the pressure put on them from both sets of parents, particularly when she found she was pregnant. Her father, a religious man, said they must do the right thing and get married. Her mother was worried about what people would say and that was the reason for moving away to this small city. Only two years later her husband left her and Beth.

So that's why Beth hadn't met her grandparents, she thought and decided to ask more of her mother at a later date.

Lisa told her daughter she was still young and there were plenty more boys to find over the coming years and to wait. To work at a career in nursing which she now realised Beth was capable of achieving.

Only Beth knew, she only wanted one boy in her life, Andy.

Chapter Sixteen
Interfering Mollie

There was a knock at the door. It was Mollie on her way to the hospital; she called to return Beth's phone and exchange raincoats.

"Hello," Beth said, surprised to see Mollie standing at her front door. "Come on in."

"I have your raincoat, Beth." Mollie handed it over with the mobile phone still in the pocket, deciding not to ask where they had been all week.

"Thanks I thought this one was a bit too big for me but I haven't felt like eating lately." Beth was trying to be polite and not to insinuate Mollie was a bit on the big side compared to her, when actually it was Beth who was a bit on the thin side.

"Barney, ok, is he?" Mollie asked as she saw him trotting through the hall.

"Come here boy," and Mollie bent down to give him a good old rub. Barney's tail went wild, flicking back and forth. He was a very happy dog here in his new home.

"He's fine, would you like a cup of tea? How about a cupcake?" Beth inquired.

"That would be lovely. Are you not on shift at the hospital tonight?" Mollie asked, following Beth through to the kitchen. Mollie was in no rush to get to work. Beth's love life was far more important and anyway she wasn't late, yet.

"Yes a little later, I'll perhaps see you there. I'm on the wards this evening," Beth replied.

"Hello, Mrs Fox, you ok, today?"

"Yes thanks, Mollie, I feel like a new woman. I'm off to the garden to sort out the weeds before it gets dark; they think they are getting the better of me but they're not."

She left the girls to chat and carried the black bin liner and small gardening fork in her gardening gloved hands to disappear out of the back door.

Beth laughed with Mollie about her mother gardening in the drizzle, after she left with Barney following at her heel.

"Mother is really getting back to her old self," Beth told Mollie who was unable to settle in her chair. Picking up a lemon cream topped cake she nervously pulled at the paper case and nibbled at the cake's edge.

Beth felt Mollie was rather agitated as she watched her across the table.

"It's a bit damp for gardening isn't it?"

Mollie was making small talk, she found it hard to be forthright in life and the subject of Paul was even harder for her.

After her second mug of tea, Mollie asked to use the bathroom and left the kitchen as Beth's mother walked in from the garden.

"Is she ever going?" Lisa queitly asked Beth. "I want to start dinner."

"It's like she is hovering, wanting to tell me something."

Mollie returned from the bathroom and said she must leave and went off in a hurry.

"That was all a bit strange." Beth turned to her mother after shutting the door behind Mollie.

Mollie hadn't been able to discuss Paul after all. Driving off, she was cross with herself and decided to catch Beth in the staff restaurant later.

"I'm going to work now," Beth called to her mother. "And I won't be back until late."

She wished she hadn't told her mother it was all over between her and Andy, because if she was able to win him back, she wasn't sure what her mother would have to say.

The evening went by as quickly as ever, always so busy in the hospital. Walking out through the hospital doors, the two women bumped into each other.

"Hi, you tired? I am," Mollie said to Beth.

"Yeh, glad I'm going home."

"Did you get to see Grace?" Mollie asked.

"Yes, she's pulling through ok. Hasn't got the use of her legs yet though and Josh was there visiting her again."

"Look I have to talk to you about Andy and that message."

"How do you know about that?" Beth seemed rather annoyed with Mollie.

"I'm sorry; it was the mix up of the raincoats."

"Oh I see," Beth said.

"Well I can talk to Andy about what I know, if you like."

"No keep out of it," and Beth ran for the late night bus leaving Mollie standing by her car which had been released from the car park after the trees were cleared away. She was pleased; she didn't like driving her mother's car.

Oh dear, Mollie thought as she drove, that didn't go well.

Chapter Seventeen
A mix of people

Mollie arrived at her day job. She signed in and went to her desk, just to check if there was anything she needed to know before setting out to a training day. This was to be held in a conference room behind the doctor's surgery a few streets across from them. Michael volunteered to drive her and another staff member, as he also had attend a meeting nearby that morning, with whom, she didn't know. He arranged to pick her up later.

Michael and Mollie were friendly enough, chatting about nothing in particular while the other person sat in the back of his car. Mollie couldn't help but wonder if he really was married to a man. She hadn't a problem with that idea, it was just she quite fancied him for herself.

Pulling up at their destination, the passenger in the back hopped out to go and collect papers from the bank; she would make her own way back later. Michael leaned nearer to Mollie and asked her out for a drink, touching her hand as he said the words.

"Around seven thirty?" he said with a beaming smile and now holding her hand, expecting her to say *yes, I would love to*.

Mollie was taken aback by this question. She couldn't think quickly enough as to what to say as she pulled her hand sharply away to pick up her handbag.

After a few seconds of silence, which seemed like hours, she replied in a firm tone.

"I don't think so, unless its just as friends."

Why did I say that, she thought it sounded strange.

Now it was Michael who was taken aback; he thought they got on well at work and he wondered what she meant by just friends.

Mollie by now was out of the car and slamming the door behind her. She daren't look at him. She mustn't let him into her heart.

He slid the car window open ready to call after Mollie but she turned and spoke first.

"Ask Victoria," Mollie called back.

With her chin up and her high heels clip-clopping on the pavement, her hips swaying, she kept walking. She was in control, she told herself.

***

"Lovely, tea and biscuits," Mollie thought as she entered the training room. She was there to update her first aid course, which she was responsible for in her office.

Tea was just what she needed and Mollie walked over to the long narrow table positioned by the wall to help herself. A circular seating arrangement was set out in front of a whiteboard which waited for notes to be written on. Leaflets and bandages lay on a smaller table close by. Bandages waiting for arms and legs of some poor unsuspecting volunteer, who would be experimented on. Mollie remembered her first attempts and smiled happily to herself; she was an old hand at all that now.

She felt a presence behind her, she turned her head and her hand wobbled a little, making her spill her tea into the saucer. It was Jack the paramedic.

"Hello there," Jack said, smiling.

"What are you doing here?" she asked.

"Assisting the trainer. Perhaps you will stand in as an injured person, then I can bandage your other arm, so you have a matching pair." He was as cheeky as ever, she thought.

Mollie liked that; in fact, she rather liked him, she thought as she found a seat at the back of the room. She didn't want to get picked out as a make-believe injured person.

The morning went well and at lunchtime, Jack came over to sit next to her with a plate of finger food and offered to share.

"Well, this is nice," he said, with that smile that half filled his face now showing crow's feet around his brown eyes and deep laughter lines at the side of his mouth.

Instead of concentrating on answering the multi questionnaire paper now given out, Mollie's mind kept wandering off to three men. Paul the doctor, who she had let go and now for some reason regretted it, Jack the paramedic who made her heart flutter, her handsome hero from the day of the storm, and Michael who she liked at work but could not understand. She had little knowledge of his private life, other than words from Victoria.

Jack was behind her, again.

"Stop doing that. You keep making me jump," and she laughed.

The pair talked about the day's training as they made their way to the front door after Mollie answered the questionaire and handed it to the tutor.

Outside Mollie saw Michael standing on the pavement next to a black Audi A3 Cabriolet car. She had forgotten at that moment that he was picking her up. She noticed he was driving yet another different car. For some reason this bothered Mollie but she wasn't sure why.

"What's the matter?" Jack asked noticing her frown.

"Nothing," she answered.

Mollie looked away from both Michael and Jack when her phone rang and she quickly removed it from her bag. Beth was calling her.

"Grace is coming round and making sense; can you get over here right now?" Beth said with an urgency to her voice.

"Can't stop, have to be at the hospital," Mollie called out as she dashed away from Jack and passed right by Michael. "Will come into work later."

"Be there in a tick," Mollie replied to Beth and shoved the phone into her bag.

Completely ignoring Michael and Jack's offer of a lift she haled a taxi. Both men looked hard at each other.

"But Mollie, I was offering to drive you, anywhere you wanted to go," Jack mumbled to himself.

Michael was also left standing bewildered. He didn't understand Mollie or her remarks from earlier. He had not been back to work to have words with Victoria, but wondered if he should, quickly deciding against it.

Mollie laughed out loud once she entered the taxi. There stood two men on the pavement watching her leave and it felt good.

Mollie arrived at the hospital ward and saw Josh holding Grace's hand. Beth stood to his side smiling. Mollie hoped he had asked her that all importent question.

"Come on, Mollie, let's go for a cuppa and leave these two alone," Beth suggested, pushing Mollie back through the door.

As the two women made their way down the corridor to the staff room, they passed a group of four people heading in the opposite direction. One of the two ladies looked very much like Grace, Mollie thought.

"Why did you do that?" she asked. "I've only just got here."

Beth apologised for snapping at Mollie and explained she thought Josh was about to propose. Mollie would have loved to have been there to enjoy the moment.

"Do you think Grace will say yes?" Beth enquired.

"Oh, I do hope so," Mollie replied in her now dreamy voice.

For a woman in her early thirties she sometimes acted much younger. People told her she was a dreamer wearing rose-tinted glasses to look at the world. She would cheekily reply to that statement with 'well, that's part of my charm,' then would laugh at herself.

"We could be bridesmaids," she added, still daydreaming.

She had this vision in her head, of wearing a beautiful, floating dress while walking behind Grace in church. A teardrop formed in Beth's eye. She thought she was going to be a bride one day, to Andy.

"What's the matter?" Mollie asked.

And Beth told her all that had happened between her and Andy, plus her mother's comments over those days away. She said it helped her to understand her mother better.

"Oh, poor you," Mollie took Beth's hand. "Don't worry; I'm sure things will work out, once he knows the truth."

"It's such a mess," Beth said and now Mollie thought it was the right time to have that chat about Paul.

"Do you want Paul back?" Beth asked Mollie.

"Oh, I just don't know anymore. I rather fancy Jack."

"No, really, he's a bit of a one for the ladies you know."

"Yes, Rosie more or less told me that, too."

"Mum told me there are lots of men out there and when the time's right, one will come along and we will both just click and not to go looking."

"She's right," Mollie told Beth and thought to herself, she must stop worrying about her own age.

She still had plenty of time to enjoy life without a man.

After their conversation, Mollie returned to the ward on her own and was surprised to see Josh surrounded by two late middle-aged couples. He quickly introduced them as their parents. Grace was sleeping once again but this time a natural sleep and Mollie took a quick look at the third finger on her left hand; still no ring. Mollie smiled at Josh and turned to leave.

"You will come back, won't you? Grace has told me a little about how you three ladies met." Josh was almost pleading with Mollie to return.

"I will," she promised him.

When Beth arrived on the ward later that evening she found Josh on his own, the parents had left. He stood to leave; he was able to walk with two sticks now and knew he would soon be discharged from this hospital, but also knew he would be back everyday to sit at Grace's bedside and wait for her to fully recover.

That little red velvet box would stay with him and go everywhere he went. He would be ready for that right moment, to ask the most important question he would ever ask.

Although he still wasn't convinced Grace would say yes.

Chapter Eighteen
Hospital Gossip

The following day Michael wasn't at work and Mollie asked around as to why. No one seemed to know where he was.

"Miss Obnoxious will know," Chloe called across the office to Mollie; she meant Victoria, of course.

"Did someone call me?"

Victoria appeared and Chloe dipped her head so as not to show her wicked grin.

Before anyone could ask, Victoria explained with that smirk on her bony face that Michael had gone to town to see his man. She carried on strutting over to the photocopying machine where two women stood talking. They quickly moved away, not wanting to converse with her.

Mollie and the others in the office raised their eyebrows and rolled their eyes at each other. No one really liked Victoria but then she didn't spend time trying to mix with the rest of the staff.

The working day ended and Michael hadn't been seen or heard of all day. Mollie worried that Victoria had made up tales and told Michael.

"Perhaps he's on holiday," Chloe suggested.

But Mollie still worried. She was on a mission to find Paul and to sort Beth's and Andy's problems out, which now seemed more important than hers.

It was one of Mollie's weekly evening shifts at the hospital and she thought that was as good a place as any to start asking about last year's Christmas party. Mollie missed it, owing to her being away skiing at the time.

It was a busy evening and the hours were ticking away before Mollie had the time to talk with her colleagues in the staff room about this Doctor Paul McCloud and when he would be starting his new role at this hospital.

A few people did remember Paul from that party. One nurse in particular commented on him being a bit over the limit with his drink, after his girlfriend stormed out.

"I think his girlfriend's name was, Victoria, yes Victoria. She was giving him a hard time all evening."

"In fact from the moment they arrived," another added.

"That's right. She left early after screaming at him for drinking too much and kissing that girl."

Everyone was now joining in with their little bit of knowledge as they passed by.

"Who was she?" Mollie was intrigued but no one stopped talking long enough to tell her.

"'*I suppose you're looking for her*'," she shouted and then left the party. She'd also had too much to drink, as I remember."

"Thats right; she stumbled up the steps when she left the hall."

"Oh, yes, she did," and a few laughed.

Mollie was surprised at all this information. Paul didn't used to drink to excess. Suddenly she wondered if he was unhappy and really had come back to look for her.

Rosie was working a night shift. She would be in soon; she would remember Paul well, as she was the oldest nurse to have worked at this hospital it seemed. She was coming up for retirement, after giving her life to nursing, at least thirty years and so far hadn't married. Mollie would stop in and talk with her, to find out where Paul was living now.

Mollie had briefly seen Paul the night of the storm, but that was a while ago now and she hadn't bumped into him since. That led her to believe he didn't live close by and wasn't out searching for her either; that made her feel sad.

Both Rosie and Jack walked into work together that night and Jack immediately thought Mollie had been waiting to see him.

"Hello, gorgeous," Jack called out as he came up close to Mollie. He was ready to place his arm around her shoulder, to give her a side hug. She moved away.

"What's up, not pleased to see me?"

"Ah, just the person I wanted to see," and Mollie took hold of Rosie's arm and they walked off together towards the staff room.

Jack looked startled. He was convinced he could add Mollie to his long list of girlfriends and his smile dropped away as he walked off, feeling deflated. Undeterred, he suddenly turned his head, put on one of his biggest smiles and called after them.

"See you later, girls."

"He really fancies himself," Rosie remarked to Mollie.

"I quite liked him, but now, I'm not so sure," Mollie replied.

"Leave well alone. You know what they say?"

Mollie looked puzzled.

"Jack the lad."

"Oh yes, very apt." And Mollie smiled to herself.

Both girls headed off for that chat before one started work and the other drove home. Rosie told Mollie about Paul's whereabouts and when he was starting work at the hospital.

"Yes, of course, you and he were an item once, weren't you?" Rosie remembered and looked as though she was trying to remember more. "Why was it you two broke up?"

Not wanting to go into the history, Mollie asked the question she was dreading to ask, was he married?

"Good grief, no," Rosie quickly replied. "He did have a relationship with a girl for a long time when studying in London. She was very weird, a bit mental if you ask me. Well so I was told."

"Do you remember her name?" Mollie asked.

"Victoria, I think, yes Victoria."

"Really?" Mollie was startled to hear the name Victoria again. It was only a short time since the staff had talked of a Victoria.

"Did you know her? What happened to her?" Mollie really needed to know more.

"No, I didn't know her personally but I heard she put about dreadful stories of Paul carrying on with people after they split up. I mean to say women and men."

"No?" Mollie sat upright in shock and stared at her friend. Paul gay or playing the field, 'no' not the Paul she used to know. He couldn't have changed that much, or was he drinking?

Mollie had a sudden thought, was Michael married to Paul? As fast as that thought flashed through her mind, the next told her not to be so silly.

Rosie loved a good old gossip and gained her information from a London nurse who had been a long time friend of both her and Paul. She was invited by him, to attend the christmas party.

"Staff nurse Rosie, are you going to stop gossiping and do some work tonight?" Sam, the charge nurse was coming through the doorway.

"Just coming," Rosie jumped from her chair.

"What was her last name?" Mollie asked Rosie as she was leaving.

"Browning. I have to be off now," Rosie smiled and turned away from Mollie.

Mollie had found out what she wanted to know, where he lived and when he was starting work. Victoria Browning was her other shock of the day. It was the same woman Mollie worked with, but Rosie couldn't tell her anything about Michael.

Mollie headed off home, thinking she would leave Victoria for another day. She also wasn't sure whether to find Paul's house and confront him. What would she achieve, or even say to him? Mollie was muddling her own mind as she drove on. She must take more time to think all this information through;

after all it really was none of her business what Paul had been doing in London for the past few years. He was no longer with her and it was Beth that Mollie worried for now.

***

Mollie wore her serious face as she bit her lip, narrowed her eyes and looked over the top of her computer the next day at work. Studying Victoria, she wondered what her game was.

"You looking at me?" Victoria's voice shouted across the room.

The rest of the office staff looked up from their computers and phones, wondering what was going on. Chloe thought this could get interesting.

"No, not really," Mollie said as Victoria marched over to her desk.

All the staff stopped working, wondering what was going to happen next. They waited with bated breath.

"Just thinking," Mollie said and shrugged.

"What do you mean, just thinking?"

Victoria was wild now, she bent over Mollie's desk and glared into her face as the rest of the staff looked on. Was Mollie going to put Victoria in her place? Someone needed to, but Mollie, of all people. She didn't argue with anyone, as mostly she was in her own world of dreams or tapping away on her computer keyboard. The strange thing was, she would stand up for other people's rights and fight their corners but not for herself.

Unbeknown to the rest of the staff, Victoria knew Michael's real standing within the company and was out to catch him for herself. No meek and mild woman named Mollie was going to have him and all his money.

Although Mollie was shaking inside she wasn't going to let Victoria see this. Mollie threw her mobile phone down on her desktop, it showed the picture of Paul kissing Beth. Mollie previously sent a copy to her own phone after finding Beth's in the pocket of the raincoat.

"How did you get this?" Victoria screamed.

She become very defensive, her whole body language was saying, 'don't mess with me'. She suddenly calmed herself, when she saw Michael coming over.

Michael came closer to see what the problem was. After all, he was the manager and he needed to see for himself what the fuss was all about. He had no time for arguments between women or men come to that.

"Now ladies, what's the problem?" he asked in a calm voice. "Perhaps we should take this into my office."

Mollie picked up her phone as Victoria tried to grab it, but Mollie was too quick to let her clear the screen.

Once in the office, Victoria let rip, like some mad person, stalking up and down. She was as white as a ghost and her bony face was exaggerated by that hair pulled hard back. She was shouting about men and how they use women for their own needs. Mollie was stunned into silence and turned to look at Michael with raised eyebrows, making Victoria completely lose control, before ending up in a flood of tears.

Michael was dealing with the situation while Mollie continued to look on, saying nothing. He eventually told Victoria to go to the bathroom and tidy herself up.

"Compose yourself, before you return," he added as Victoria left with a tissue held to her face.

Chloe and the rest of the staff were still watching, getting cross if a phone rang and deciding to ignore all calls as this situation was a lot more interesting.

Michael phoned and requested tea which was always a good thing in an English situation. In a crisis make tea, Mollie thought.

A rather smart woman wearing a bright red suit appeared and placed a silver tray of tea and biscuits on the side table. As she leaned over in front of Mollie, she was able to read her company name badge.

Jane. Personel assistant to Mr M Walker.

She stepped towards Michael, passed him a letter and quietly requested he signed it before taking it with her as she left the room. Mollie noticed this but could not ask about the woman before Victoria returned.

An hour passed by with Victoria doing most of the talking, mainly about Mollie having a sordid affair with Paul while he was engaged to her, Victoria, and living in London together.

Rosie hadn't told Mollie this piece of information. *'They lived together, engaged?'* Mollie kept quiet. Victoria was digging herself a big enough hole without her help.

"She chased him, you know," Victoria went on, while pointing at Mollie.

Much more was spoken of before Michael again picked up the phoned to asked for a taxi, to take Victoria home.

"Take some time off and go to see a doctor and not Doctor Paul McCloud," Michael told her.

Mollie barely dared look at Michael. How much of what Victoria spilled out would he believe?

When Victoria left, Mollie stayed for a second cup of tea. She was actually quite shaky after hearing all Victoria's lies. Mollie knew her relationship with Paul finished years before he met Victoria. It meant nothing to her now as she realised she didn't want him back but it mattered what Michael would think of her. They were interrupted by a phone call before she had a chance to speak.

Mollie sat in his office and looked around as he took the call. She hadn't actually taken the time to look around before and she was surprised at the elegance of the room, holding a few very expensive art pieces which were either hung on the walls or sitting on the green leather top of his large oak desk. These items reminded her she wasn't in a shop trying to buy a man to marry. She must take no notice of her mother either, who said to go find a rich man. No, she needed to go with her heart, not her head and love would find her someday; suddenly she was sure of that.

Michael replaced his phone and wanted to know about Paul and Mollie's relationship but felt he wouldn't be so bold as to ask her.

Before Mollie could ask Michael about the rumours of him being gay, he asked her out for dinner.

"Tomorrow at eight?" he said with confidence, again expecting a yes.

But her father's funeral was tomorrow.

"No!" she said sharply and ran from the office for home. She was now near to tears herself and couldn't handle any more that day.

Michael was unsure what he had said to upset her. He stood watching her leave the building from his office window before the phone rang again. He was being called upstairs to see the company chairman on a business matter.

As Mollie ran from the building, many thoughts crowded her mind. To think Victoria said all those awful things about her and Paul and to Michael of all people!

Mollie had lost her beloved dad. She couldn't let Michael into her life or she would only get hurt again and Paul, she lost him long ago through her own doing. Jack, well that was unlikely to ever take off.

More questions were forming in Mollie's mind after the conflict which had just passed, including *Jane, personal assistant to Michael Walker*. Why would he have a personel assistant when Victoria was his assistant office manager? Mollie needed to know more about this person who worked on the top floor. She had called him 'sir' when she handed him a letter to sign. So many unanswered questions rolled around in Mollie's head as she rushed from the building feeling embarrassed.

She drove home and knew she needed to see Andy as soon as possible, to explain about Victoria's attempts to ruin peoples love lives.

Suddenly she remembered Grace in hospital and a thought crossed her mind. She could move away and meet new people. Perhaps that was her answer, maybe thirty-four years of age was not too late to change her life, Grace was thinking of doing that very thing.

Arriving home she remembered tomorrow, cross with herself for forgetting. She'd been waiting two weeks for this day to arrive and suddenly it was here, she didn't know how she was going to cope with saying goodbye to her beloved father.

This final act reminded her that life was for the living. At last she wasn't feeling desperate to find a man, no she could live with or without a man.

Chapter Nineteen
Say Goodbye

Mollie arrived home to find Michael standing on her doorstep, next to the empty plant pots. The summer flowers now completely dead, just like her dad, those pots had been his pride and joy.

"How did you get here so quickly?" Mollie asked Michael, forgetting the time she had spent in a layby, to wipe her face and pull herself together, a place where she often stopped to think, where she sat and tossed over so many things in her mind. That layby was her place. Today it had been thoughts about the woman with the tea tray, someone who only worked for the Chairman or the vice chairman of this company.

Victoria had covered most of her thoughts, though. Fancy saying all those dreadful things, trying to ruin her life and of course her mixed up feelings for Paul.

"Let's go and have some lunch," Michael suggested, as he looked sympathetically at her.

Mollie decide there and then she would; it was better than going into the house with her mother at that moment and having questions fired at her.

Chloe told Michael of Mollie's father's death and knew she needed a little comfort and Michael wanted to give it. He understood how she felt at that time. He had lost his mother not so long ago and his father was a poor old thing these days.

"Just give me five minutes to sit in the car and reapply my makeup," she told him.

Once Mollie was composed she took his open hand to help her from the car and thanked him.

The pair decided to walk the ten minutes around the corner to where a taxi rank had been set up some years before. Both Michael and Mollie needed some fresh air after the morning they had had and after a short walk, their cars left behind, they were driven to the edge of the city in a black taxi cab.

Arriving at Alison's coffee shop they ordered ham and cheese toasties. This was the best way to relax, Michael thought as he also ordered a cappuccino for Mollie and for himself, a hot chocolate. His drink arrived with cream swirled around on top, with tiny pink and white marshmallows sprinkled on the top of that. Mollie's eyes glared down in amazement at the glass mug, wondering if he really was going to drink its contents. To think he was so tall with a well-shaped body, not an ounce of fat was showing anywhere as far as she could tell. Her eyes moved over him. A naughty thought popped into her mind, she would like to see his six pack.

Michael's shape, Jack's muscles and then she remembered the old man on the beach and chuckled to herself; he had no six pack and his wife knew that too.

"That's better," Michael said as he took a mouthful of his drink, leaving cream around his lips. He liked to see her smiling face.

"Do you work out?" Mollie suddenly blurted out without thinking. Stop it, she thought, he is not a free man. "Oh! Sorry, I shouldn't have been so forward." Mollie realised what she'd said and dropped her head.

"Well sometimes," he smiled back at her, almost teasing her and Mollie felt embarrassed. She really shouldn't have asked. Michael realised he had embarrassed her and changed the subject. They chatted, getting on very well, she thought, but Mollie wouldn't ask about a wife or a partner. She didn't want to hear the answers. If he did have either she would rather not know and Michael didn't mentioned Paul. Victoria was the main topic as Mollie just couldn't bring herself to talk about her father at that moment.

Jealousy must be Victoria's problem, she tried to explain to Michael. Mollie was spilling out everything she knew to him, from the Christmas party to Victoria's involvement with sending Andy the photo of Beth being kissed by Paul and all the other rubbish Victoria spoke of in the office. She stopped talking, dropped her gaze. Poor Mollie despaired of herself.

Michael listened intently, as he had to Victoria. He was a good listener.

"Do you think Paul hoped to bump into you, Mollie?" Michael at last asked her.

"Maybe."

She began to think perhaps Paul had returned for her after all. Rosie said she thought he may have. This seed began to grow in Mollie's mind but did she want to go back in time? After all, there was a hero in Jack who was hanging around. He kept chatting her up, not that she told Michael this.

Michael sat across the table from her right now and he made her heart flutter whenever she looked too long at those sparkling green eyes. Then there was always Ben, her friend. Did any of them fit into her life right now? Perhaps not. She felt herself becoming confused again, she frowned and knew she must leave; she stood up.

"What's wrong?" Michael asked smiling at her.

"Nothing. I have to go."

"I'll take you home. You can take the rest of the day off and the week too, to help you with tomorrow."

That was the first time he had mention her father. She smiled at him. They both left the table after Michael paid. Mollie thought how kind and thoughtful he was, but still, she knew little about this man. As they walked, she asked if he was going to work that afternoon. Michael said he wasn't as he was meeting someone.

"He'll be wondering where I've got to," he added.

"Oh, yes, of course, I have heard," Mollie instinctively said.

Immediately she thought it was his gay lover.

"You have?" Michael asked with a worried look on his face."You know then?"

"Well, yes, the whole office knows, it's nothing to hide," and Mollie smiled.

Michael's middle years showed as he frowned his deep lines on his forehead. How did people know? He felt quilty that he failed this man after his mother died and didn't want people to know.

"I have to be going, he'll be waiting," Michael told Mollie as he left her at her door.

So he does have a man hidden away somewhere, Mollie thought.

The pair said their goodbyes. He wished her well for the funeral and gently kissed her on the cheek, as a good friend would, before leaving. Her heart made a massive jump, her cheeks turned red and she could not move as she watched him drive off.

***

Michael drove with a heavy heart as he thought of Mollie losing her father to death; he was losing his father, in a very different way, to dementia which was getting progressively worse. Guilt set in long before he moved his father into that care home; he really couldn't care for him any longer in his own place. He couldn't leave him on his own either. His father kept asking for his wife which disturbed Michael greatly as he still missed his mother. When Michael went to visit him, his father didn't recognised him anymore and that also hurt him deeply.

***

Mollie now sat on the doorstep daydreaming about that kiss. It was warm and tender and Mollie hugged herself, shut her eyes and pretended Michael was there with her and was about to do it again. *He would ask her out on a date, she would say yes.*

She was brought back to reality as Patch pushed her head into her arm. Mollie stroked the old cat, picked her up and they both went indoors.

That night Mollie lay in her bed thinking about many things. The day to come and how she would cope and if Victoria was telling the truth about Michael being gay. He hadn't tried to kiss her on the lips, so maybe. And that photo her mother hid away in her handbag.

Sleep eventually came to Mollie.

Chapter Twenty
A Sad Day

Mollie made a few last calls to check everything was in place for her father's day.

It was a cold morning with the sun peeping through the late autumn clouds and as Mollie looked out of her window, she felt he was watching her. The white clouds would soon be replaced by grey, it would rain later, the weather forecasters had predicted. She'd better take her raincoat, even though it wasn't black.

She remembered the times as a child when she and her father made pictures in those pretty wispy clouds that slowly changed shape as the wind carried them across light blue summer skies, and Mollie cried as she thought she saw his face form in one.

Her love for her father was as strong as a daughter could have for her father. He gave her his unconditional love and she had loved him back. He was always there for her, played with her as a child, talked to her about careers and boyfriends as she grew, more so than her mother, who seemed to have no time for her. What she was going to do without him, she had no clue. She wiped another tear away.

So many little girls want to marry a man like their fathers, she thought.

Mollie remembered Beth. She didn't have a father. Then in a flash, an idea came to her as she sat back on her bed eating breakfast. But that thought would have to wait for later and Mollie made her way over to her mirror.

She looked at herself, wondering where her life was going. Her father's life was gone. He achieved much but not everything he wanted; she wasn't sure if anyone ever did. Funerals made people stop and think about their own lives, she knew that now. Mollie straightened her black and white dress, slipped her feet into her black shoes and a short black jacket. She was ready with tissues in her black handbag.

The flowers, peace lilies and white daisies, his favourite, arrived with a solemn-looking woman from the florist shop.

"Sorry for your loss," she said, leaving Mollie standing in the doorway feeling lost in herself while holding a wreath. Mollie hated those few words, '*sorry for your loss*'; they sounded so cold and empty, why do people say them? It's like people who say '*have a nice day*'; they couldn't care less if you did or didn't. They don't know you.

Mollie was finding fault with everything at that very moment in time and it was so unlike her. After all, she had enjoyed the Americans saying those words when she was out there on holiday a couple of years back. She had smiled at the words they used in place of the ones she used at home, like the day she found a heap of crisps on her plate after she ordered a burger and chips. Mollie actually found a smile appearing on her lips but it was short lived. She liked traveling. Maybe she really did need a change of scene, she thought again. Perhaps she would move away.

Then the door knocker hit the wood once more. The long black shining hearse was parked in the road and a man in a top hat stood at her door. This is it and Mollie took a deep breath, walked into the hall and stood for a second before opening that door. She called to her mother, who had said nothing for the last three hours. Mollie went to find her, she was sitting with Patch on her lap. Mollie took hold of Patch, put her on the floor and took her mother's hand, a rather alien feeling for her, as they were not a touchy-feely pair, but now was not the time to hold bad memories and she slowly led her mother to the car.

There would only be the two of them in the car which followed her father and Mollie was at a loss for the right words to say to her mother. Her throat felt tight, she was unable to talk. The backs of her eyes stung with the building tears.

There were a few friends of her father's from the factory already seated in the church pews when Mollie and Margaret arrived with Ben. Barney, well he had escaped yet again and now sat at the huge oak church doors. A dog's love for their master will live on and so he had found his way there to watch the coffin pass by. Mollie had no doubt of the dog's love.

Mollie and Margaret walked the crimson carpet to the front of the church to take their places; they passed Rosie. She had nursed that man in his last few hours of his life and Mollie was grateful. The congregation stood, the old wooden benches creaked. Wife and daughter both tried to control their emotions. Margaret was trying to understand how her once young husband, so virile and strong, now lay in that coffin old and grey. The daughter cried knowing he wasn't there, that only a worn out old body lay quietly inside that wooden box. His soul now returned to a better place. Mollie was a believer, well she would be, she was a dreamer after all and she liked wearing her rose tinted glasses.

The service went well, considering so few people attended. People tried to sing hymns but the words got stuck in their throats making the atmosphere worse. Sniffing could be heard in this ancient building and Mollie found she could not give the eulogy for crying. Margaret took over and still she showed no emotions as she spoke the words.

As the people left the old church, their feet could be heard rustling through the crisp fallen autumn leaves around the church yard. Mollie remembered how as a child she held her father's hand and skipped and kicked her way through the piles of leaves at this time of year, when really she was supposed to be helping him gather them up in their garden; what fun she had back then.

Mollie saw Beth in her raincoat and pink wellingtons just outside the church doors. She was holding onto Barney and Mollie smiled at her.

"I need to see you, but not now Beth, not here. I will phone you; it's about Andy," Mollie whispered as she passed by.

Beth looked concerned; she wouldn't sleep that night for wondering what Mollie might tell her.

The day came to an end and Mollie was emotionally exhausted by the time the few family members left the coffee shop which Mollie had hired for the afternoon wake. Old Uncle Arthur and his wife Ethel arrived late from up north, after their train had been delayed.

Aunty Flo, Mollie thought, she really had managed to show herself after some odd twenty years. They weren't a close family by all accounts.

Mollie kicked off her shoes after returning home and laid back on her sofa and as she shut her eyes she heard crying from her mother's bedroom. Mollie sat up sharply to listen, wondering if she should go to her mother. She felt compassion for her now and knew deep down she loved her. After all, she was her mother and she hadn't hurt her physically. She just seemed indifferent to her most of the time and often mentioned she would have liked to have had a son, even giving him a name.

Perhaps if she had had a brother or sister her mother would have been different towards her. Mollie now knew she wouldn't experienced the love of a sibling.

Maybe she really did need a change of job, in a new town. To get away. Wasn't that what Grace was looking for, a new life? But she couldn't leave her mother right now.

Chapter Twenty One
A Coffee Shop Meeting

The office was a happy place since Victoria left and Mollie returned after her two weeks of compassionate leave. Oh, how Mollie fancied Michael as he walked passed her and stopped to enquire as to her well being. She held her breath to stop the butterflies rising. She smiled at him.

"Fine, thank you," and turned to her keyboard, her head down as though to work, when in fact she was checking her diary. She wanted to arrange a coffee shop meeting for the coming Saturday afternoon. She knew who she should invite and sent out the messages by text. Now she only needed to wait and hope everyone turned up at their allotted time.

She was putting in place that flash of an idea which came to her as she lay on the sofa the morning of the funeral, the plan she hadn't explained to Beth at the church door.

***

Saturday morning arrived and Mollie had heard back from all the people she had invited. All could make their different time slots. Not one of her friends mentioned to the other about Mollie's invite as she had asked them not to, only explaining she needed to speak with them away from work.

Mollie arrived early and sat herself down at the head of a long oblong table at the rear of Alison's coffee shop, which she had reserved. From her position, she could watch the car park and the door to see each individual arrive, all part of her master plan. She would greet each one and offer them a coffee. This was like a military operation to Mollie: it must be just right on the day. There was a reason for the staggered times which would become apparent to her guests as the afternoon wore on.

The first to arrive was Josh in his casual jeans and jumper, his police uniform packed away while he made a full recovery. He missed his training in Scotland and decided against the three months work experience too. He wanted to stay by Grace's side. Still, he hadn't found the courage to open the red velvet box, telling himself he would, once she was well again.

After his release from the hospital he had wanted to meet the surgeon who saved both his and Grace's life and they were the two people to arrive first. Paul was following Josh through the door.

Mollie greeted Paul with a kiss on the cheek and felt a flutter inside. Was that a good or bad thing for her? She wasn't sure as her hand touched his cashmere sweater. He was dressed casually in dark blue jeans which clung tightly to a small backside which looked rather good as he took his coffee to sit with Josh.

Mollie admired Paul for his work, but admiration did not constitute love, she thought as she watched the two men in deep discussion.

There would be one last surprise for Josh at the end of this afternoon, again arranged by Mollie.

Mollie needed to know how she felt about Paul and if there might be a future. Actually she was still none the wiser on that score. The most important reason for Paul attending was that photo on Andy's phone, not for her to sort out her life. Andy reqiured an explanation from him.

No one noticed Jack sitting at the coffee bar next to another man already drinking a hot chocolate with all the trimmings. Both sat with their backs to Mollie's little gathering and had already introduced themselves to each other. Jack wore a cap pulled down to his eyes and a scarf pulled up around his neck and chin, both of which were not out of place with the howling winter weather outside. He ordered his coffee in a quiet voice so as not to draw attention to his northern accent. He had overheard Rosie at work talking to another member of staff about a meeting she was attending. Rosie was a gossip and knew a little about a lot of things, so she was useful to have there too, Mollie decided.

Now it was Beth's turn to arrive. Mollie was going to play peacemaker and Cupid at the same time, not knowing if either would work out how she wanted. She was determined to reunite Andy and Beth by the end of this day.

Beth walked in and looked around at these people she knew sitting and chatting between drinking coffee. There were now two plates of cupcakes in the centre of the table as Mollie knew Beth loved a cupcake. Mollie helped herself to one lemon cake, but for once Beth was more interested in the group of people rather than the cupcakes.

"Come on in, Beth, come and sit down." Mollie pointed to a chair close to her and ordered Beth a coffee.

"What's going on here?" Beth asked as she marched up to Mollie.

"You're part of the hospital and know everyone, don't you?" Mollie felt a little awkward and ignored her question.

"Well, yes, but what's he doing here?" Beth was now pointing at Paul.

Mollie made no reply. As Beth went to sit she looked around and saw Andy arriving.

"What? I'm leaving," Beth scowled at Mollie as she pushed her chair back, scraping the wooden floor, which caught everyone's attention. She turned to glare at Andy and then back at Mollie. For a moment Mollie thought Beth was going to scream at her but she didn't.

"Now, Beth, keep calm," Mollie started to speak. "Paul and Rosie have something to tell Andy. Paul, you explain about the Christmas staff party," Mollie instructed him.

Beth sat down with her arms crossed tightly over her chest and now Andy stood to stare at Mollie, not sure as to what to say to his hostess.

"Will you all sit down and talk to each other." Mollie was very stern in her voice.

Paul was the one with the answers and he was ready to give his apologies. Rosie was chipping in with the little she remembered from that party night. When the subject was finished, Andy stood to the right of Mollie while Beth sat on her left. She asked for another strong black coffee with sugar this time.

"But what about Victoria and those words she sent to me, along with that picture?" Andy was still very cross and wanted to know more of why Victoria should want to do such a thing, after all he didn't even know her and how did she get his number?

"Sit down." Once again Andy was put in his place by Mollie, the woman who would normally walk away from confrontation.

Paul started talking again about his relationship with Victoria and again Rosie added her information regarding Victoria's move back to the area and taking a job where Mollie worked and the reasons for that. As to how she came by Andy's phone number, no one seemed to know.

Victoria had decided that if she couldn't have Paul, then Mollie wasn't going to have him either and Mollie's friends became caught up in her vengeance.

Mollie's cheeks flushed and she fidgeted in her chair. She didn't know what to say with Paul sitting opposite her. This afternoon wasn't supposed to be about her and Paul or Victoria come to that. But Paul wanted everyone to know the evil streak that woman had.

Jack swung around on his stool and pulled his cap off and his scarf down to show a silly grin on his face.

"Well, this is all very interesting," he interrupted.

Rosie glared at Jack from her seat close to Mollie.

"Did you follow me here?" Rosie asked.

"Oh, do shut up," Jack said and laughed at her.

"Have you come back for Mollie, Paul?" Jack turned to face Paul. He wanted to know who she might pick, thinking he was in with a chance.

"Well, have you? Michael asked too as he also swung around on his stool positioned next to Jack. He faced the gathering at the table now and looked Paul straight in the eye.

"Well?" Michael repeated.

All this time Mollie sat stunned, not uttering a word. She wanted no eye contact with either man, she was so embarrassed and suddenly sprung to her feet. She shot a hard look at Paul, waiting for his answer and then she scanned the faces of the men and women she had invited and the two she hadn't, Michael and Jack.

After all she was the one who arranged this meeting to help her friends sort out their love lives, not hers. Only now all eyes were on her, was Paul here to find her, his Mollie? That's what he had called her all those years ago, in the early days of their relationship.

So far Paul hadn't replied. That made Mollie feel even worse, did no one want her? Suddenly it dawned on her, she couldn't go out looking for love, it came to find her. And she ran to the door, not wanting to hear an answer from any man.

"What are you doing here?" Mollie stopped and turned back to ask Michael, her whole insides shaking as she held onto the door handle.

"I often call in here, for my comfort drink after my emotional visit on a Saturday afternoon."

He stopped before he said more, and there, in his hand was his hot chocolate with all the trimmings.

"Why didn't you bring your gay partner with you, then?" Mollie blurted out.

Everyone in the coffee shop went deadly quiet as a few placed their drinks down in slow motion and others stopped in time, cups held at mouths. Alison stopped moving between her customers and was now like a statue. She couldn't believe her ears. She had often seen Michael in her coffee shop since his return from New York, she wouldn't have thought him to be gay.

"Oh, the man I visit. He's my father. He's in a care home." Michael suddenly realised what people had been thinking. Mollie died a little more inside, as a low current of voices spread around the shop. It was to get worse for Mollie. "And the wedding ring?" he went on. "Well that was given to me by my wife. She died in a car crash."

Before Mollie knew the outcome of Beth and Andy's relationship she was running from the coffee shop in a flood of tears, with Michael chasing after her.

This was the second time she ran from Michael after something stupid had been said. The last time was after Victoria and her outburst in his office and now, here in this coffee shop, in front of so many people she knew. The chatter grew as people chewed over what had just taken place. There was much to talk about, from the weather storm, to love and its storms.

Alison's head was spinning from watching all her customers swinging around on stools, standing up and sitting down. Wow, what a different Saturday afternoon to the normal teenage thing; now here were middle aged people acting in the most bizarre way in her shop.

"I didn't think Michael was gay, far from it," Rosie added, as if she knew. Now she would have lots to gossip about; Rosie was in her element.

Everyone was sitting in a daze around the table while Alison was thinking 'it all happens in here,' and kept on selling coffees. This was so good for her profit margin.

Jack confirmed that when Michael and he sat together at the coffee bar listening to Mollie's little gathering while pretending they weren't there, Michael had told him he was married to an American girl who was killed in New York.

Michael returned to finish his cold chocolate and to tell Jack he lost sight of Mollie. Her car had been left where she parked it. He would go to her home, he told Jack who had sinced moved over to sit close to another young woman and was in the throws of chatting with her.

Beth looked hard and long at Andy as Michael left for the second time.

"Wheres he going?" Andy asked anyone who would tell him. It would be Beth.

"Well if you don't know, what sort of a man are you? If you don't recognise love and how to chase it."

"Oh," Andy replied sheepishly.

Andy moved closer to Beth, grabbed her by the waist, lifted her from the chair into his arms and kissed her so hard on her red painted lips that they almost turned blue as the blood stopped circulating. She felt she could have melted in his arms.

"I'm so very sorry. I acted like a kid." Andy uttered the words from a lip-stick covered mouth as he let her go.

"Yes you did." Beth whispered in his ear.

"Will you marry me?" he said as he dropped down onto one knee, forgetting where he was and all those people watching.

"Yes, oh yes, I will," Beth shrieked and threw herself at him, forgiving him in an instant.

Everyone in the coffee shop clapped and cheered.

"Now that's how you chase and get your girl," Andy said as he punched the air and nodded his head at Josh. Beth had told Andy about the red velvet box.

Everyone laughed, there was so much joy in the building that Mollie's friends had already forgotten about her outburst and that she was no longer there.

Andy would have to take Beth shopping for a ring, as he may have been thinking of asking her one day, but just, not today, this he did spontaneously, he smiled to himself; he normally planned his life.

"More coffee everyone? It's on the house." Alison called out.

What did I just say? On the house. Oh no, that's my profit gone and Alison smiled to herself. She really didn't care, she was so happy it happened in her coffee shop.

The door opened and a surprise guest arrived, the last one on Mollie's list. Silence fell once again, everyone turned to look, a gasp seemed to leave each and every mouth.

Grace sat in a wheelchair pushed by Alan, Jack's partner at work. He borrowed a ambulance to bring her to Josh who walked up to her, bent down and kissed Grace lovingly. Instead of standing up again he pulled from his pocket the little red velvet box, and flicked the lid open.

"Will you marry me?" he asked.

Grace glanced around the room, everyone held their breath, wondering if she would accept.

"Yes, I will," she replied, grabbing Josh by the neck to pull him close and kiss him again.

Both Josh and Grace gazed into each other's eyes. True love had eventually found them. The noise of the cheering could be heard by shoppers down the road.

"Who's staying to celebrate?" Josh asked.

Everyone said a very loud "YES! We are."

Andy told Beth they would shop for a ring after the coffee party broke up. In the mean time Michael drove over to Mollie's house. Both missed the excitement in the coffee shop.

Margaret told Michael that Mollie wasn't there and did not invite him in.

He was sad for Mollie, for she had missed the excitement which came about from all her arrangements. He hung around outside for sometime but eventually gave up and went home, thinking he would catch her at work next week.

***

Many hours later Mollie arrived home. She dashed in through her front door, leaving it to swing open as she rushed up the stairs to her bedroom. She slammed her door behind her. She still felt humiliated. She had run to the park in town and hidden under a weeping willow tree which still stood after that storm. There she had sat on damp ground, her arms tight around her knees and letting her mind drift. Later she walked and walked for hours, having lost Michael down a side road.

"What have I done?" She had cried out loud to the pair of swans on the river. She remembered swans mate for life, why couldn't she find a mate for life? Be settled, be happy. Once she thought she had found her love in Paul. But now she knew she'd messed things up and she had to get away.

The noise she made on her return to her home made her mother jump and Patch fly off Margaret's lap. The old cat took Margaret's knitting, caught in his paws, around the room, around chairs and table leg, knitting wool got entangled everywhere.

"Whatever's happened?" Margaret shouted up the stairs after Patch chased passed her and almost tripped her up. Paws skidding up each step, he dashed, to hide under Margaret's bed. But Mollie

- 153 -

wasn't coming out of her bedroom ever again, not even to see what the meowing and shouting was all about on the landing.

After a few hours Mollie pulled herself together, packed her suitcases and thought, thank goodness it was Saturday and she didn't have to work tomorrow. In fact, she decided there and then to resign and leave town that very night and not workout her notice. What could the company do? Only fire her.

By late evening her suitcases stood in the hall ready to go.

"Where do you think you're going?" Margaret asked. "Leaving me on my own, now your father's gone."

"Sorry mum, I have to go. I have done something really stupid, made such a fool of myself," and her tears readily reappeared.

The taxi beeped outside. Mollie struggled with her cases, the driver placed them in the boot while she told her mother she would write once she was settled.

Not taking her car meant Josh's friends in the police force couldn't trace her, she thought. Mollie wouldn't have known that they cannot trace people or cars unless they are involved in a criminal case.

Margaret stood at her front door and watched the taxi move off.

"But Mollie, take care. *I love you,*" she called after her daughter.

Mollie didn't hear and she didn't look back.

Chapter Twenty Two
Beth needs to find Mollie

The long damp autumn turned to winter and Beth changed her clothes around to wearing her thick winter coats and boots, hats and gloves. She rummaged in her wardrobe for that new pair of jeans when she noticed that raincoat stuffed at the back and it brought many memories with it. Mollie helped Andy and her greatly before she disappeared and it still worried Beth as to where Mollie might be right now.

Buying that raincoat had brought new friends into her life. That coat had history joined to it and she remembered the phone in the pocket situation.

Beth was happy to be planning a wedding for next year and being offered a training place at the hospital also gave her much to look forward to. Her young school days had finished. She now took on more books and courses, exams and hands-on nursing work. All her worries gone after she received the results required to pursue her career, to become a proper nurse.

"That's the wedding dress I would like," she said, turning to look at Barney.

There was just a hint of sadness in her voice. She wanted Mollie to see her in that dress but no one knew where she was.

Beth looked through yet another book of wedding dresses. Barney cocked his head to one side and peered at her with that knowing look that animals can give, while humans wonder if they understand. Beth was talking to a dog who brought love into her home, a dog that had once belonged to Mollie and again she wondered.

She must try to find Mollie, to help her, but no one seemed to know where she had vanished to after her outburst in the coffee shop.

Beth had visited Michael who was also desperate to find Mollie. Nurse Rosie knew nothing either when Beth approached her. That was a surprise to Beth, as normally Rosie knew all the gossip. Even Paul couldn't help and then the day before New Year's Eve when it was icy on the roads, Jack attended a call out and there he heard a whisper. Attending a young girl at a roadside incident, she asked him where the woman was who helped her. A woman named Mollie with a pale blue V W Beetle car. She stopped to call the emergency services.

Jack wondered if that woman could have been the Mollie he knew; after all he knew she drove a car of that discription. He phoned Josh who was now back at work in the police force. The temptation to put a trace on the car was extremly strong as this young girl remembered the registration number. But could he do that without a lawful reason, he wondered.

Margaret had recently told Lisa, that on Christmas Eve Mollie left a card and gift for her on her doorstep. She saw Mollie collect her car and drive off as she watched from an upstairs window. Margaret hadn't told anyone other than Lisa, who she swore to secrecy.

***

Rosie screamed with delight, "Happy New Year!"

Many friends were gathered around Rosie who was the life and soul of the party.

Josh stood by the wheelchair as proud as any man holding Grace's hand out to show to the world the ring on her finger as he announced the wedding date was booked for early spring.

The empty red velvet box had left Josh's pocket, at last, to be tossed aside in his sock drawer.

Grace missed the chance of that job after her long stay in hospital but she didn't care anymore and Josh, well, he decided to stay in the police force. He was in another post, in a different city where they could both start afresh together and make new friends.

Andy held Beth closer when Paul came near and then eyes moved to Jack who came bounding through the doors of the hall to join the loud group who were singing at the tops of their voices.

"Rosie, Rosie, I have to tell you." Jack stopped in his tracks at the sight before him. Two girls flashing engagement rings at him was very scary. These wedding plans might be catching. *I had better watch out*, he thought.

"Hi, Beth, look at you two."

Jack laughed as Rosie pulled him close for a New Year's kiss.

"Now what's so important, Jack?" Rosie asked releasing him from her bear hug.

"Rosie. There's been a sighting."

"What are you going on about?"

"Mollie."

"Really, come on tell me more."

"That's what I came to tell Michael."

"Is Michael here?" Beth interrupted.

"Yes, I invited him. Well, he knows us all, doesn't he?" Rosie seemed put out at the question. Why shouldn't she invite him and he had accepted thinking Mollie might show.

"Come on, where is she?"

"Well that's just it."

"What do you mean?"

"She has been seen. We just have to locate her."

Chapter Twenty Three
Weddings

The weeks and months past.

The search for Mollie had taken place. The men had got together and found her. She was back living with her mother, Margaret, but did not return to the office or to her hospital work. She was changing her life, spending time searching for a place of her own to live in and another job. She was also arranging weddings with her two new friends.

Late spring arrived. The church was full to its sides. Pink cherry blossom hung from trees lining the old churchyard's path as a bride strolled slowly by with her head full of dreams for her future. Smiling, she entered the church through the open oak double doors where the Reverend Sommerfield stood in his white robes. The sun was blazing through a stained glass window at the far end of this pretty little church, which had witnessed so many other services over its many hundreds of years, but today was the most important day in this bride's life and she was heading to the altar, where her man awaited her.

The choir boys stood ready to sing.

There were flower arrangements of white daisies and pink roses placed at the ends of each pew, at the entrance to the vestry and on stands just inside the church doors, leaving an aroma that filled the air with sweetness alongside the chitter chatter of happy people, many of whom thought they wouldn't see this day.

"You have to feel sorry for anyone suffering from hay fever," Rosie chuckled to Jack who still managed to escape any woman tying him down to marriage, even if Rosie had tried too.

Jack's mind was full of playful thoughts as he studied Rosie's dress. She looked like a strawberry to him in her long red and floating dress which rounded out over those rather large hips, and with a green bodice plus the yellow flowers in her red hair, he made his comparison but wouldn't say. He loved her in his own way and wouldn't hurt her.

Hats of many colours, shapes, and sizes wobbled on ladies' heads as they moved around in anticipation of the bride walking past.

A smiling Margaret was there sitting with Lisa. Neither had a man in their lives to escort them but they seemed happy enough together as good friends. Both shopped together for their outfits. Lisa brushed at her dress of pale green trimmed with a wide pale pink belt at her now narrow waist. Her weight had reduced with a lot of hard work and encouragement from Beth. Her newly styled hair showed off her pink hat which sat like a small plate to one side of her head. Beth's mother was feeling well again and moving through her menopause with the help of HRT. She had promised Beth she would do her proud and she had.

Lisa looked across at Andy and smiled at him. She even liked Andy these days.

Margaret wore a rather smart flowered patterned cream dress and plain cream short jacket which she complemented with cream shoes and clutch bag. Her hat was something else, the fashion world would say, like a flying saucer of cream netting and flowers.

Josh stood close to Andy, both in their suits feeling all bundled up, wishing they could get back to jeans and tee shirts. Andy fiddled with his collar as Josh nudged him to get his attention.

"Beth's mother came around to liking you then?" Josh stated, having noticed the smile.

"Yes, who would have thought it. Beth is so pleased," Andy replied. "I get invited to the house for meals these days, you know." Andy carried on with, "she also told me that you got married to Grace."

"Did you really?" Doctor Paul interrupted the two men standing close to him.

"Yes, I did. Here, look at the photos," and Josh pulled out his phone, clicked onto one picture, leaving a ping sound echoing around the old church.

"Put that away, son," the Reverend Sommerfield said as he walked passed the men on his way to stand at the front of the church and wait for the bride to arrive at the altar. He was ready to carry out the service.

The Reverend Sommerfield smiled as he passed the line of men. He dropped his head as his thoughts turned to this young generation. They had some strange ideas.

Why are Five men standing inline, in the front pew, awaiting a bride, when only one will marry her?

Having lowered the phone to his hip, Josh was still able to show Andy and Paul the photo of Grace sitting in a wheelchair outside the registry office back in early March. It had been a low-key affair, Josh said; that was what they wanted, just parents attended. Her wheelchair had been decorated with daffodils and she wore a long lemon dress which covered her bandaged legs and with a white fur jacket to keep the chill of winter at bay, she held a bouquet of snowdrops with more dotted in her hair. In the photo she was holding her hand forward to show off her wedding band, now sitting next to that sparkling diamond ring from the little red velvet box. She looked radiant on her day as the bride today did.

"Yes I'm married, and to think Andy, the boy who said he wouldn't marry, will soon wed Beth and with her mother's blessing, who would have thought it?" Josh grinned in jest as he said the words and put his phone away.

"And you Paul, not married quite yet, then?" Michael asked. He also stood in line with the other men.

"I hear you are the vice chairman of the company," Paul enquired.

"Yes, that's right."

"You kept that quiet," Jack pitched in.

"Now boys, lets have a little hush, the bride is on her way," The Reverend Sommerfield said.

Both Margaret and Lisa now wondered at the sight of the bride as she arrived, before looking across at the line of men.

"Why are all her men friends standing together?" Margaret asked Lisa.

"Quiet Margaret, the Vicar's coming over."

"But which one is the best man?" Margaret kept asking.

Lisa didn't answer.

The bride was about to glide slowly from the church doors between her friends and family to one of those men.

All the important men in the bride's life stood side by side at the front of this church in matching suits with small pink rosebuds in their buttonholes.

***

Alison came rushing in at the last minute, having been working all morning in her coffee shop. She was invited after so much romance had happened in her place.

Rosie discreetly pointed Alison out to Jack who looked rather dashing in his black-tailed suit, pink shirt, white tie and silver waistcoat, which matched the other men standing close by.

The ladies become friends and so had their men over the months of Mollie's disappearance.

"Look what Alison's wearing." Jack laughed with Rosie. "She's a coffee in disguise."

Her two-piece suit was mainly of a coffee colour trimmed with cream lapels and buttons. Her accessories were of cream, extremely high-heeled shoes, and small cream bag. A fine cream netting over a box-shaped hot chocolate coloured hat that hardly fitted her head.

"Where're the marshmallows?" Jack commented, cheekily looking at Michael and winking.

"Stop it." Rosie got the giggles just as Alison turned to show the other side of her hat. There sat a small group of pink, silk marshmallow shaped trimmings.

"Oh!" Jack called out as Rosie buried her face in his shoulder to cover her giggles.

"Look here she comes, behave you lot," Michael said, as the bride eventually moved off with her bridesmaids following.

There had been a hold up at the church door because of the sudden shower of rain that arrived as the bride left her car. The two bridesmaids had their hands busy holding a *beige raincoat* around the bride's shoulders to keep her glittering dress dry.

The three women, Beth, Grace who was holding onto one walking stick, and Mollie, all giggled side by side, for they knew how a storm brought them together and how they eventually laughed about owning the same style raincoats.

"Rosie, what's going on?" Jack asked.

"That's where it all started, three women with the same raincoats, meeting in a storm."

Who would have guessed the connections made that day not so long ago. Friends made for life.

The organ started to play the wedding march.

All eyes were now on the bride as she moved off. She looked like all brides, gorgeous in her long dress of lace over silk. Her crystal-studded veil held back in a sparkling tiara clipped into her blonde curled hair. Shuffling noises came from the many feet in the church as everyone stood to attention. Jack stood upright and beamed with pleasure to see the beautiful bride looking so very happy. The music played, the choir boys sang and the bride glided up the crimson carpet towards her bridegroom. He turned to admire the woman who would soon be spending the rest of her life with him. Her dress dazzled him as the sun cauglt the crystals. Tiny pearl buttons made a line down from her neck to her waist and on down the train to its end. Lace sleeves met in a point with her hands which held a small posy of pink roses, some open, others in bud and white daisies with just the smallest of greenery tucked in between.

The last time Mollie stood in that church, she held a tissue to catch her sad tears, the day she said goodbye to her father. Today she could feel his spirit standing next to her. How she wished it was him holding her arm but it was her lifetime friend, Ben. He was giving her away and she was pleased, for they loved each other in a very different way.

Josh nudged Paul who poked Michael in the side and all three smiled.

Michael stood tall and straight with the biggest smile of all on his handsome face. He held out his hand to take hold of Mollie's. Ben passed Mollie's hand to him after kissing it.

"I love you, Mollie," Michael said as he looked into her eyes.

Now she could look into his and smile, "I love you too" she said. Followed a little later by both saying the soft words of,"I do."

The End

Thank you for reading Storms and Happy Endings. I hope you have enjoyed it.

Don't miss book 2 – Some Love Never Dies

Writing as Jasmine Appleton:

Katie's Magic Camera Series

Printed in Poland
by Amazon Fulfillment
Poland Sp. z o.o., Wrocław